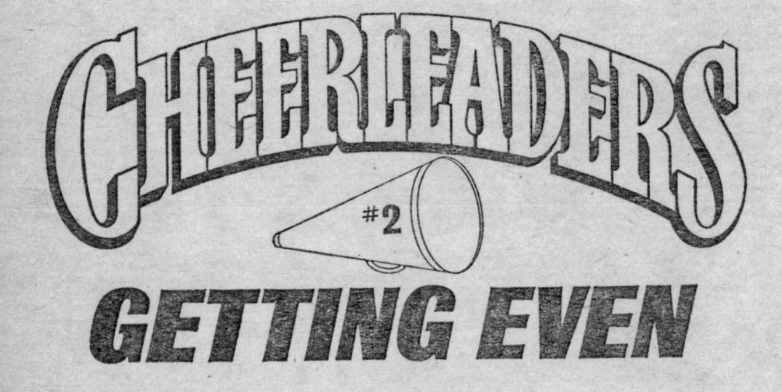

GETTING EVEN

CHRISTOPHER PIKE

SCHOLASTIC INC.
New York Toronto London Auckland Sydney Tokyo

ISBN 0-590-33403-4

12 11 10 9 8 7 6 5 4 3 2 1   2   5 6 7 8 9/8 0/9

Printed in the USA   01

CHEERLEADERS
GETTING EVEN

CHEERLEADERS

Trying Out

Getting Even

Rumors

Feuding

All the Way

Splitting

CHAPTER

The blazing sun didn't know that summer was over and school was back in session. The high humidity had turned the suburb of Tarenton into one big sauna. Fortunately the girls' locker room was cool and quiet, and Mary Ellen Kirkwood was able to fix her hair and face. She had enough on her mind. In a few minutes she would have the honor of being the master of ceremonies at the first pep rally of the new school year. Why last spring she had wanted to be captain of the cheerleaders, and *enjoy* such privileges, was beyond her at the moment. What was she supposed to say, anyway?

"Hi, my name's Mary Ellen and these are my good friends: Nancy, Angie, Olivia, Walt, and Pres! We're here to share with you the excitement we have for our fantastic football team!"

In her mind's eye, she could see rows and rows of bored faces.

"Before we get started, we'd like to welcome all you new freshmen! Let's have a big hand for the kids!"

No one would clap. A few heads would begin to nod.

"We sure are glad to have you all here! And we sure are glad to be here, ourselves! Right now we'd like to show you a routine we worked hard on all summer and performed in cheerleading competitions!"

A handful of knowing students would smirk. They would be the ones who knew how badly they had scored at camp with the routine. About this time, she would begin to freak out.

"But we'll need your help! When we sing the chorus, 'We are the Wolves! We are the Wolves!' we want you all to growl at the end! Can you do that? Great!"

The six of them would launch into the routine. When the part came where they did interwoven cartwheels, she would miss a beat and bang into Angie Poletti and Angie would bang into Olivia Evans and Olivia would bang into. . . . The crowd wouldn't growl, they would laugh.

"Are you worried about what you're going to say?" Angie Poletti asked, standing beside Mary Ellen at the locker room mirror, applying lip gloss while simultaneously munching on a Snickers. Angie's boyfriend, Marc Filanno, refilled the school vending machine and was allowed to take as much candy as he liked, much to Angie's delight and grief. She had to work to keep her weight down.

"No," Mary Ellen lied, trying to get her hair

into some style she didn't hate. Most people saw her as the classic blonde, blue-eyed beauty, and her confidence in her own appearance was relatively solid. That is, until she looked too long in a mirror that also held Angie's reflection. Though the two were cast from the same mold — tall, long legs, shapely hips, lithe upper body — Angie was supposed to be plain. It was an established fact. One could give her picture to a hundred guys and over ninety of them would say, "Yes, this girl is definitely plain." But in person she looked great! It was her smile, Mary Ellen realized — it had energy. Mary Ellen decided she would have to work on her own smile.

"You have to make the audience feel wanted," Angie said. "Ask how their summer was."

"My speech is already prepared."

"And tell a joke," Angie continued, not listening. "Humor's always safe. Joke about how lousy we did at camp this summer."

"We'll see." That was the *last* thing Mary Ellen would say.

"I like those earrings," Angie said, wiping a smudge of chocolate off her lips. "Gold suits you. Where did you get them?"

"My mom bought them while on vacation." Mary Ellen saw no point in mentioning that they weren't real gold and that her mom's week off in August had been partly spent shopping at the local J.C. Penney's where she'd picked up the earrings on sale for $3.50. The Kirkwoods were poor in an affluent town. Mary Ellen's father had a bus route and her mother was a clerk. They lived in a turquoise house that Mary Ellen hated, away from the fashionable parts of town.

Angie's mother (her dad had died in a construction accident when Angie was a baby) was no tycoon, running a marginally profitable beauty parlor out of their home, but Mary Ellen disliked anyone knowing she herself was poor.

"Where's Olivia?" Mary Ellen asked, changing the subject.

"With Nancy."

Mary Ellen checked her watch. Five minutes and they would have to head for the gym. Her nervous stomach would be in good shape by then. "Where's Nancy? And don't tell me she's with Olivia."

"As a matter of fact . . ." Angie laughed. "They're both probably around somewhere, inside the boys' locker room. Nancy wants Coach Pulera to tape her ankle."

"Is that necessary? Everyone will be able to see it from the stands," Mary Ellen said with annoyance.

"Her sock will cover it," Angie said defensively. "And what if the tape *does* show? If she needs the support, she needs it."

Mary Ellen kept quiet. Nancy Goldstein and Olivia Evans were fellow squad members. A few weeks earlier, during a practice session the day before camp competition, Nancy had twisted her ankle. Everyone had made a big fuss over it, especially when Nancy had insisted that she would compete the following day, but Mary Ellen couldn't help noticing that the foot hadn't swelled much, if at all. After they had competed and done poorly — due largely to Nancy's lousy timing — she had had to wonder if Nancy hadn't simply prepared an alibi, knowing she might mess up. Of course, this was an opinion she kept to herself. Nancy was really all right, and it wasn't her fault that her father was a successful lawyer.

At that point, Mary Ellen and Angie's conversation ended. It was seldom that the two of them spoke for any length of time. She liked Angie enough, but she just couldn't understand someone so carefree. The world was such a mess that it didn't seem right that Angie should be totally happy. It seemed unnatural.

Mary Ellen concentrated on her eye shadow. Whenever she was in front of a mirror, she could never decide whether she had on too much or too little makeup. She was overly concerned with her appearance, she knew, but what did a model have outside of her looks? And she *would* be a model — Brooke Shields, look out — just as soon as she graduated from Tarenton High and bought a one-way ticket to New York, where she intended to become a huge success.

Suddenly the locker room's doors popped open, bringing a wave of humid air, and Nancy Goldstein and Olivia Evans.

"The pep rally's going to start a few minutes late," Nancy said, athletic tape peeping an inch above her right sock. Her tan was beautiful, her skin practically as brown as her big panda bear eyes. Nancy had sunbathed half the summer away at her pool and Mary Ellen realized she was envious . . . and wished she wasn't. She *wanted* to be accepting and generous. One day she, too, would have money, lots of it, and wouldn't have to spend June through September pedaling her bicycle around a hick town like Tarenton.

"Why?" she asked, wanting to get her speech over and done with.

Nancy shrugged. "Some of the freshmen are still searching for the gym."

"That's ridiculous," Mary Ellen said. "You can see it from almost any point on campus."

Angie laughed. "But have you seen some of those freshmen? Some couldn't see over the school's hedges. They look like munchkins, like . . ." her eyes brightened on Olivia, "like our hobbit, here."

Mary Ellen waited to see how Olivia would take the joking comparison. The extreme opposite of Angie, Olivia was deadly serious, almost as if all of her life were a job where the boss was always watching. Mary Ellen supposed having a series of heart operations at an early age could put a dent in one's playfulness. Perhaps to Olivia even an ordinary day was nothing to be taken lightly. Mary Ellen still hadn't figured her out, except that she wasn't a sickly child anymore. Though she was small and delicately built, she could outlast the lot of them.

"My father called me a hobbit yesterday," Olivia said quietly, brushing aside a strand of reddish-brown hair from her deep-set, dark eyes. "I must read those books and see if I'm being complimented."

"You are," Angie reassured her. "Hobbits are cute, except for their feet, which are supposed to be hairy." Angie could get away with such remarks.

"Speaking of feet," Mary Ellen said, feeling an obligation to ask, "how are yours holding up, Nancy?"

Nancy caught Mary Ellen's eye briefly before answering, as if to say, *I know you think I'm a phony*. But it was only an impression, and Mary Ellen wondered if she wasn't being too harsh on Nancy.

"Coach Pulera said beginning next week, I shouldn't have to bother with tape."

"That's a shame," Angie said. "You won't have an excuse to go into the boys' locker room."

Nancy blushed. "He puts the tape on in his office, not in the locker room."

"But his office is *in* the locker room," Angie said, "and I hear it has big windows."

Nancy began to protest, but Olivia interrupted, muttering, "They're not that big."

"Ah, hah! Did you see anyone?" Angie pressed. Essentially they were all sex maniacs, Mary Ellen decided — even Olivia.

Nancy was regretting having even mentioned Coach Pulera and his tape. "No! I didn't look. Listen, we've got to perform in a few minutes. I don't want to have another locker room rap session."

"When did we have the first one?" Mary Ellen asked, enjoying Nancy's discomfort.

"I don't remember. *One* is one too many."

"For goodness' sakes," Angie said, "we're *in* a locker room! What other kind of rap session are we supposed to have?"

Nancy sighed. "This is ridiculous. There were no boys there at all."

Olivia nodded. "There was too much steam to see."

"*Steam*?" Angie's eyes widened. "Now we're getting somewhere. Where there's steam, there's a hot shower. And at least one —"

"All right! All right!" Nancy told the ceiling "There were windows. There was steam. There was someone in the shower. But —."

"Who was it?" Angie interrupted, laughing.

"I don't know!" Nancy yelled. "I didn't have my contacts in!"

"But you did at least *try* to look?" Angie wanted to know.

Nancy was exasperated. "Why are you asking only me? What about Olivia?"

Olivia shook her head. "The windows were too high for me to see anything."

Mary Ellen frowned. "Wait a second, Nancy. You don't wear contacts."

Nancy began to speak, thought better of it, turned a deeper red, and burst out laughing. "Maybe I should get some! I tried as hard as I could and I couldn't see him at all!"

"*Who*?" Angie yelled.

"Pres!"

That broke them all up, even Olivia. Preston Tilford III was gorgeous — never mind that he was also a member of their squad. In the midst of her giggling fit, Mary Ellen wondered if she shouldn't sprain her own ankle and get it taped regularly. Last year, despite her dropping hints of her availability, Pres had pretty much ignored her. Once they had parked in his car. She had responded to his kisses because she knew that was what he wanted, but in reality he hadn't excited her at all. There were none of the overwhelming feelings she had when Patrick Henley just touched her hand. During camp she had caught Pres more than once staring at her. . . . There was hope. Besides being handsome, his family was rich; his father owned Tarenton Fabricators, which was not a liability as far as Mary Ellen was concerned. In fact, money was what interested her the most about Pres . . . and money was also what Patrick was missing.

In the middle of their laughter, something that rarely occurred among the four of them and an event Mary Ellen took as a favorable omen for the new year, Mrs. Engborg burst through the doors.

"What are you four carrying on about?" she demanded. Ardith Engborg was their squad coach. Rumor had it that she had been a drill sergeant in Vietnam. Mary Ellen questioned the rumor only as to which side she had been on. She could be one strict lady. To her, cheerleading was a sport — not an excuse to socialize, not a display of beauty and sexuality. Tarenton High's excellence in cheerleading competitions — four state titles in the last ten years — had begun the year she had taken over. A small but wiry woman, her powerful voice made them jump.

"Nancy just told a great joke," Mary Ellen said quietly. She respected Mrs. Engborg, but she wasn't sure if she liked her.

"Tell your jokes *after* the pep rally," Mrs. Engborg said, striding back and forth in front of the short row they had automatically formed. "This will be the first impression you'll have to make on the school, and first impressions are the ones that count. If they don't like you today, they won't like you all year. Angie, wipe that chocolate off your face. Nancy, pull your sock above that tape. Olivia, don't look like you're going to a funeral. Mary Ellen, do you have your speech prepared?"

"Yes, ma'am."

"You had better. I told Mrs. Oetjen, our beloved principal, that this year's squad was the one to watch. If you say anything foolish, your role as squad captain is over, understand?"

"Yes, ma'am." That meant she would have to rewrite her entire speech.

"I didn't see Walt or Pres outside the gym. Where are they?"

"I saw Pres taking a shower in the —" Nancy began, grinding to a miserable halt. Mary Ellen did all she could not to burst into laughter. Angie didn't even try, and her laughter surely would have infected the rest of them if Mrs. Engborg hadn't promptly intervened.

"Close your mouth, Angie," she said. Angie did as requested. Mrs. Engborg continued, "So that was your big joke, Nancy. Very well, if you don't find Pres or Walt in the gym in exactly five minutes, you have my permission to drag them both out of the showers. Now I have to leave you fine girls and take my place in the stands with the rest of Tarenton High's faculty." She paused as she opened the door, adding in a less gruff voice, "I'm sure all of you will do well."

"Thank you, Mrs. Engborg," they said in unison, sighing in collective relief as the door shut behind their coach. Angie forced the remainder of her Snickers in her mouth. Olivia went back to looking far away. Mary Ellen searched frantically for the blandest possible speech. Nancy plopped down on the bench, angry.

"I wish you hadn't mentioned that I was the one who was telling jokes," she said.

Mary Ellen could not believe Nancy was blaming her. "The joke telling wasn't the problem," she replied coolly. "It was your peeping at Pres."

"I was *not* peeping at Pres!"

"Oh yes, I forgot. You didn't have your contacts in."

"Come on, girls," Angie broke in. "We were laughing about it a minute ago, let's not start fighting about it. Go ahead, kiss and make up."

Mary Ellen knew Angie was right, but she also thought how naive she had been to consider their shared joke a good omen. Nothing had changed between Nancy and her over the summer — the friction was inevitable. *Why* was not clear to Mary Ellen.

Is it just because I'm jealous? she wondered. Nancy did have it easy. While *she* had to study a couple of hours every night to get good grades, Nancy breezed through her classes. When Nancy graduated, her parents would pay for whatever college she wanted to attend. Mary Ellen knew her parents were hoping she could help with the bills when she got out of school. Financially, they were definitely from opposite sides of the track. But if jealousy was part of the problem, maybe it was a two-way street. Mary Ellen tried to think what *she* had that Nancy must want. Nothing came to her.

Try another theory, she thought. Maybe they didn't get along because they *had* to get along. While performing, they were as dependent on one another as a newborn baby on its mother. Perhaps if they hadn't been so suddenly thrust into a pressured situation, they would be better friends. Actually, when she took a step back from their trivial bickering, she realized that she liked Nancy. Nancy was no slouch; she had a lot of admirable qualities. Time would probably smooth out their rough edges. At least Mary Ellen hoped so.

"I take back what I said," Mary Ellen said.

Nancy looked up in surprise at the sincerity in her voice. She smiled faintly. "So do I."

"Great. That wasn't so bad," Angie said, wadding up her candy wrapper and scoring two points in the garbage can. "Now let's go. Our fans are waiting."

CHAPTER

As they walked to the gym, beads of perspiration quickly formed on Mary Ellen's forehead, as much from nervousness as the heat. Their school was located on a slight hill in the old part of town, commanding a superb view of Narrow Brook Lake. Tall, ageless trees, mostly oaks and elms, rimmed the cool, flat expanse of water, thinning as they progressed through to the campus. The Georgian brick buildings were gathered in a huge C shape, surrounding a wide courtyard interlaced with lovingly maintained flowers and hedges. Yet the beauty of the surroundings did nothing to set Mary Ellen at ease. It was old hat, and when her head was in knots, every place was a lousy place to be. She lagged behind the others, wishing for a hotline number to the President's speech writer.

"Hi, my name's Mary Ellen! I'm a cheerleader and so are these clowns! Please love us!"

"Hey, Mary Ellen!"

It was Patrick Henley, hurrying her way in green coveralls. As was often the case when she saw Patrick, she didn't know whether to smile or grimace. Oh, she liked him — Attila the Hun probably would have liked Pat. His warmth was all but irresistible, and he was certainly worth looking at — a strong hunk, a shade over six feet, with curly brown hair and perfect features that would have been intimidating if not for his semi-permanent grin. If she hadn't known Patrick, had simply seen him on the street, she would have wanted to know him. He invoked that kind of gut reaction. Unfortunately, he worked for his father and his father was Tarenton's number one garbage man. How could she, a prospective Cover Girl, go through the entire school year with a trash man for a boyfriend? It was impossible. She would have to tell him, "I like you as a friend. That's all." If only he wasn't a lot more than a friend to her. But just looking at him made her yearn for him, and almost destroyed all her hard-fought-for cautiousness.

Patrick had pursued her all last spring. Right before summer vacation, she had offended him by rejecting him one time too many. Finally she called him and apologized. When he asked her out again, she had weakened and gone with him. Their first date was memorable. He picked her up in his garbage truck. He hadn't made any plans, just asked what she wanted to do. They saw Stephen King's latest movie and topped it off with an enormous pizza. What was surprising was that she had so much fun! Patrick was a vortex of energy and life. When he tried to kiss her goodnight, she didn't resist. Indeed, she subtly demanded more than she ever had . . . even from Patrick. She had wrapped her arms around his neck, and returned his kisses with the same passion with which they were given. They didn't pass the point of no return, but having Patrick's arms around her made it easy to fantasize what it would be like beyond that mystical point. His touch was delightfully gentle, perfectly rough. It took a long time to fall asleep that night.

After that, Patrick kept insisting that they go out again, but Mary Ellen refused, over and over again. She knew that if she kept seeing Patrick, kept letting him kiss her the way he had — and *wanting* him to — all the plans she had made for her future would be forgotten.

Reflecting back on that one night, Mary Ellen wondered how she could continue refusing him. Who could replace him? Pres? He didn't even seem to like her — at least not the way Patrick did. But, Pres was every bit as handsome, if in a less heart-stopping way. He also drove a red Porsche, and his hands were never dirty.

"You look fantastic!" Patrick said, moving to hug her.

"Don't! Your hands are dirty." She cringed, taking a step back, knowing that his hands were perfectly clean. "You'll mess up my uniform."

"I just wanted to wish you good luck," he said, taking the rejection in stride.

"Thanks," she muttered, feeling guilty. The truth of the matter was, she still wanted to see Patrick. She just didn't want anyone to know it.

"Will you wave to me? I'll stand in the back row, right in the center."

She paused. "I can't. Mrs. Engborg would throw a fit."

"Is it okay if I wave to you?"

"Just don't growl."

"Do you have your speech prepared?"

"Oh, heavens," she whispered, momentarily holding her head up with her hand. She hadn't even got past the, "Hi, I'm Mary Ellen!" He touched her shoulder.

"Are you mad?"

"No! No, I'm . . . I'm nervous." She looked up at him, feeling that pull to him. What she did next went against all her internal rationalizing. "Give me a kiss for luck," she said.

He did so. It was *not* a quick kiss. His arms went around her. Momentarily forgetting where she was, she hugged him back. He lifted her off the ground and she could feel his strength — and she had no desire to resist. It was like the first time. Better. His lips took the place of the world. Nerves at the base of her spine that were usually asleep woke up. His nearness filled her head and her heart, stimulating her imagination with delicious possibilities.

Wait a second, she thought, this is a public place! She pulled back, smoothing her red and white pleated skirt. "I've got to go."

"I'll be cheering for you."

"Don't," she called, hurrying to catch Angie and the closing gym doors. The kiss had helped. She felt more confident. This would be fun! *I'm a cheerleader . . . the best.*

* * *

"Should we go in and get Pres?" Olivia Evans asked. They were standing outside the boys' locker room, an identical counterpart to the girls' locker room. They had checked and Walt was already inside the gym ready to perform. Pres must be taking an awfully long shower. It wasn't like him to be late.

"Mrs. Engborg was only joking," Nancy Goldstein said, watching Mary Ellen adjusting her skirt. Nancy didn't begrudge Mary Ellen having to host the pep rally, but in practically every other respect, she was envious. Mary Ellen Kirkwood was a tall, gorgeous blonde. Nancy Goldstein was a short, pretty brunette. Mary Ellen always seemed calm and contained. There were few things Nancy didn't fret over. Mary Ellen received good luck kisses from her boyfriend. Nancy didn't even have a boyfriend.

Nancy had just begun to recover from a wrenching romance she'd had in the spring. She had fallen totally in love with Rick French, who had rushed her for ten wonderful days . . . until his girl friend, whom he had never mentioned, came home from boarding school. Then everything had ended, and Nancy had struggled with humiliation and rage and rejection. Now she was feeling whole again, though there were still moments when she ached to be held and kissed by Rick again.

Last year she had dreamed of having a large circle of friends. This year she would have been satisfied to have a handful of close friends, or even just one *boyfriend*. Except for a brief vacation in the Caribbean, summer had been boring, with days spent reading in the library or sitting at home waiting for Rick to phone.

"We're running out of time," Olivia warned.

"I know," Nancy said. Last spring, when they were trying out for varsity, she couldn't have imagined that Olivia would end up being kind to her. Her sprained ankle had brought them together. Probably because she had suffered so much as a child, Olivia had sympathized with the pain the injury had brought. Still, she couldn't say she knew Olivia well — whether Olivia was comfortably content or desperately miserable. Olivia volunteered few personal insights. "Are you sure Pres isn't already in the gym?" Nancy asked.

"Positive," Olivia said.

The gym floor, where the band and pep squads were presently gathered, was separated from the audience by a huge, flexible wall that would roll up like an accordion when Mary Ellen gave the word. Mary Ellen would wait for the rest. Theoretically, they had time. Of course, if they waited too long, they might end up performing to a very small crowd.

"I'm going to try shouting," Nancy said. "Pres! Pres! That guy's either still in the shower or else he's deaf."

"Excuse me, is that the gymnasium?" a soft English voice asked.

Nancy turned to find a young man approximately her own age with short, bleached hair and a face that belonged on the cover of a teen heartthrob magazine. His jaw was strong, his mouth large and seductive. Even in the glaring sunlight, his green eyes were striking. Her immediate impression was one of depth; the boy radiated intelligence. He was not particularly muscular, his loose white silk shirt and bright red pants did not hide his thinness, but he was at least six feet tall and his firm posture indicated that he worked out. A gold earring glittered in his right ear.

"The gym?" she repeated. "That's it right there."

"I thought as much," he said in a melodious voice. "Thank you."

"Thank you," she said, realizing she had nothing to thank him for, and feeling foolish. She watched him glide toward the gymnasium, hardly touching the ground. "What do you think?" she whispered to Olivia.

"He has a nice voice."

"Doesn't he? Have you seen him before?"

"No."

"He must be new in town. He looked like David Bowie's cousin."

Olivia nodded. "He had on an earring," she said tentatively.

Nancy suddenly felt defensive. "All the guys on the videos wear jewelry. These days, it's not that unusual."

Olivia shrugged. "I don't mind what he wears."

"I'm sorry, I shouldn't have snapped at you."

Olivia raised an eyebrow. "Do you like him?"

"I don't know him." Not that that answered the question. She liked John Travolta and she wasn't exactly on intimate terms with him, either.

The way this boy looked was enough to spark her interest. "Look, he's coming back. Oh, no!"

Olivia nodded to herself. "You *must* like him."

"I guess I'm too late," he said cheerfully, walking past them. "The place looks filled."

Nancy had the irrational thought that she would never see him again, and that it mattered a lot. "Wait!" she called. He turned, smiling. Now what, she wondered? "Could you help us?" she managed.

"If I can."

"Another member of our squad is in there." She pointed to the locker room at their backs. "He's a boy, and we don't want to go into the boys' locker room. We have to perform in a few minutes. Could you maybe go in there and tell him to please hurry?"

"What is his name?"

"Pres! Actually, Preston Tilford III, but we just call him Pres for short, you know? He's blond and has a good build and a deep tan. He's. . . ." She paused to catch her breath. "He should have on pants and a white sweater like ours with this big 'T' in front."

"Sounds hard to miss." He disappeared through the metal doors.

"I wonder what his name is?" Nancy thought aloud.

"Ask him," Olivia said. A long two minutes went by. Finally the boy with the Hollywood face reappeared, shaking his head.

"There's no Pres in there."

Nancy turned to Olivia. "But you were positive he wasn't in the gym?"

"I still am."

The boy pointed toward the gym. Pres was waving frantically. Somehow they had missed each other. Seeing he had their attention, Pres jogged toward them.

"Is that him?" the boy asked.

"The one and only," Nancy muttered. "I guess we better get inside. Thanks for finding him."

He chuckled. "I would say *he* found *you.*" He turned away. "Have fun."

Suddenly, she was afraid he'd disappear again. "We could get you inside," she said.

"Come on!" Pres yelled, hand on the door of the gym. Olivia began to run toward him.

"Hurry, Nancy!" she called.

"Do you want to come?" she asked, running backwards after Olivia.

"Why not?" He quickly caught up, the two of them racing side by side. "What's your name?"

"Nancy Goldstein. What's yours?"

"Alex Hague."

They found their way inside. Her heart, already beating fast from the short dash, began to pound. Every member of the Pompon Squad, band, baton twirlers, JV Cheerleaders, and her own squad was staring at them. They were late. What a great way to start the new year, she thought gloomily. But Alex lifted her spirits with a simple remark.

"Isn't it great to make a grand entrance?"

She nodded, directing him toward the least conspicuous corner and hurrying to where Mary Ellen waited by the mike. "We were waiting for Pres."

Mary Ellen was not impressed. "Is that all you were waiting for?"

Here we go again, Nancy thought. One would have thought since they shared similar goals — to excel in school, to be popular, to be superb cheerleaders — they would have been each other's best supporter. Neither of them were on the squad solely to raise Tarenton High's level of enthusiasm for the football team. They both wanted the social benefits and the chance to perform in front of huge crowds. Maybe that was the problem. They were after the same treasure at the end of the same rainbow, and they were afraid there would only be enough for one of them. Nancy knew if they could just get over this initial hump, they hadn't worked together too long — they would be all right. For the sake of the squad, they had better get over the hump.

"You saw that gorgeous guy I walked in with?" she said, taking a chance on honesty. "I was talking to him."

It worked. Mary Ellen smiled. "Get in place, Nancy. I'm going to give the signal. Tell me about him later."

Nancy positioned herself between Angie and Walt Manners, who wagged his megaphone at her as if it were a big, scolding finger. Walt was the other male member of their squad. His features were large and powerful, his hair dark and wavy. From a distance he appeared intimidating, but close up the magic of his face immediately put strangers at ease, a perfect stand-in for a department store Santa Claus at Christmas. Though far more nimble than any guy on the football team, he was as husky as the biggest offensive linesman. He never stood still. He had perpetual "caffeine jitters," and he didn't even drink coffee. Most people labeled him a comedian, and he was forever playing pranks. His parents were important in Tarenton, hosting a morning talk show that attracted a lot of celebrities in every field. Walt was show biz, just like his mother and father.

Like Angie, he was on the squad purely for fun. Occasionally, however, Nancy thought they underestimated his complexity. It was not something she could pinpoint — perhaps just a look in his black eyes that gave the sign that deep inside his gears were turning in unexpected directions. One day, Walt would surprise them all.

"Who's your new boyfriend?" he asked.

Nancy laughed. "Just some dude I picked up in a bar at lunch."

Mary Ellen gave the cue. The bass drum started a low, steady beat. Simultaneously the partitions began to separate. What seemed like an ocean of people quickly unfolded. The horn section joined the drummer, hitting on the first notes of the Beatles song, "Got To Get You into My Life." The band, which was split in two and bunched in the corners, began to stream onto the floor. By this time, their squad was dancing, a simple "hand clasp, leg kick" routine that demanded only that they remain synchronized. Behind them, the baton twirlers and JV Squad followed their lead. It was all merely a warm-up, but Nancy was glad for the cushion before their more difficult number. All these people watching took some getting used to. She knew it wasn't so, but it seemed like they were all staring at *her*.

The song ended and the crowd clapped. It was a good sound to hear. Mary Ellen skipped to the microphone, her smile bright. Nancy had her own smile glued firmly in place. Where was Alex?

"Hi, how ya all?" Mary Ellen waved easily. A few pests yelled, "Bored!" but the majority responded favorably.

Mary Ellen continued. "There are a lot of faces out there I don't recognize from last year! You must be our freshmen! I remember my first week at Tarenton!" Half the crowd groaned sympathetically. "It was pretty rough!" The audience laughed. "Tarenton High's a great place to go to school! We have the best of everything: the best teachers, the best football team, and the best cheerleading squad!"

They chuckled again. Mary Ellen was on a roll. Nancy had to admire her cool. "But before I introduce our principal to tell you how high we rank academically, and before I bring out our football coach to tell you how many teams we're going to stomp on this year, our squad would like to put on a quick show for you! Of course, we're going to need your help! Don't worry, you don't have to learn anything, you've just got to have rhythm!" Mary Ellen raised her hands to the mike and began to clap, saying, "One! . . . two, three, four. . . . One! . . . two, three, four. . . . One! . . . two, three, four."

The audience was in the palm of her hands — literally. Soon the gym was reverberating with the beat. Quickly, Mary Ellen fell back as they formed into a "T" with Walt at the junction point, Pres in front of him, Angie and Mary Ellen holding the ends, and she in the middle with Olivia at the front tip. Normally they performed to music, but this was Walt's idea of involving the audience. The start was very simple. While holding their pompons aloft, they stomped the gym floor to the beat with their feet. For Nancy, it would have been simple if her ankle felt a hundred percent. The pounding shot stabs of pain up her right leg. Coach Pulera had explained that her sprain had been unusual because, while she had torn little tissues and had a minimum of swelling, she had significantly stretched the ligaments. In other words, she suffered a lot but had nothing to show for it.

Nancy was moving instinctively, too fast for thought. Had she had a chance to pause and consider where she was and where she should be, she would have made an error. Mrs. Engborg repeatedly hammered upon this point in practice, "*Don't think. Do*!" She was aware only of whirling through the air, spinning on her toes, and clapping her hands. The pain in her ankle was forgotten.

The next part of their act brought Walt and Pres level with one another and widely spaced. Using the guys as vaulting horses, and impersonating Olympic gymnasts, Olivia and Nancy approached from opposite sides, picking up in five steps the speed necessary to somersault over the guys. Landing beside each other in a neutral zone, they shouted, "Tarenton!" before quickly getting out of Mary Ellen and Angie's hot-on-the-heels way. As before, they repeated the cycle, throwing in variations: swapping partners, linking arms in the middle, and twirling. Nancy began to feel dizzy, but the sensation was not unexpected and she didn't panic. Time was as blurred as the stands.

They finished by forming a small pyramid, close together; Walt and Pres established a solid base, with Angie leaping onto their backs and Olivia and Nancy helping Mary Ellen on top of Angie. The structure was at best unstable. Snatching pompons from the pile, Olivia and Nancy came in from the sides and hopped onto Pres and Walt, holding onto Angie with one hand, the other hand waving a pompon. Mary Ellen was perched at the top, sweating and praying that no one had the urge to sneeze. They held this pose about ten seconds. That was a *long* time.

The crowd erupted in loud applause. Mary Ellen came off the top effortlessly and skipped to the microphone. Nancy wiped at the sweat on her forehead. Her ankle was throbbing, but she felt fantastic! They hadn't made a single mistake! Mary Ellen tried to speak but the applause drowned her out. This is how rock stars must feel, Nancy thought. It gave her a great rush, a genuine high.

So what was the matter?

"I told you we have the best cheerleaders!" Mary Ellen breathed. The guys on the football team, occupying the first five rows, growled. Mary Ellen threw them a pompon. "Hey, these are real wolves! Calm down, boys! Mrs. Oetjen wants to. . . ."

Nancy only half listened, her excitement quickly diminishing as she tried to pinpoint what was bothering her. It came to her quickly. The routine they had just performed was identical to the one they had performed at the end of camp — the act that hadn't impressed the judges one bit. Yet here the crowd had responded enthusiastically. It could be argued that today they had the home court advantage, but that reasoning only went so far. The problem, Nancy realized, was very simple. In camp they'd had competition, and those other schools had been more exciting. The realization was not pleasant. If they were to succeed at the State Cheerleaders Competition in three weeks, drastic changes would have to be made. Unfortunately, she had no idea what those changes should be.

When it was all over, Mary Ellen gave out the time and location of the next game — it was forty miles away, no one would be there — and thanked everyone for stopping by. Fifth period started in five minutes. For Nancy that was biology with Mr. Creol. In his book, cheerleaders were not exempt from tardies, pep rallies notwithstanding. Collecting her megaphone, she slid through the throng toward the door. She was two steps outside the gym when an unmistakable voice called her name.

"Nancy!"

It was Alex! Wading through the crowd, he made his way to her side. Though exhausted, she managed to smile.

"Did you find a place to sit?" she asked.

"Yes, when things started cooking, I slipped

off the floor and squeezed in with the football team. I can see if I want to be popular, I'm going to have to learn to growl."

He spoke easily, as if being popular was totally unimportant to him. Being popular was one of her main reasons for existing. Reflecting her lack of confidence, she asked, "It was pretty boring, huh?"

"Not at all. I enjoyed myself. I especially liked when your squad was onstage."

"Thanks." They were heading in the direction of the classrooms, the crowd beginning to thin. His small compliment did wonders for her. Nevertheless, a long pause hung in the air before she could think of something to say. "You're new here, aren't you?"

He smiled. "Did my accent give me away? Yes, my family only moved here from London in July. Dad had to follow his firm. I thought I was properly enrolled in school, but when I came in Monday, they said, 'Who arc you?' It took till this morning to sort out the paperwork."

"So this is your first day?" If she had had to start school in a new country four days late, she would have been a nervous wreck. Alex looked like he could have been on a picnic.

"Yes."

"I'm new here, myself. I mean, my family only moved here last year from Ohio." And I still haven't adjusted, she thought. "What class do you have now?"

He pulled a wrinkled blue card from the back pocket of his bright green pants. "Biology, Creol, SB 17. Do you know where that is?"

It was fate. It was a good karma. It was luck. She didn't care what it was, it would be neat having him in class. "That's where I'm heading now," she said with forced casualness. "Just follow me."

"I seem to be doing that already," he chuckled.

"You haven't missed much. Creol takes a week to explain his grading curve. Today we start on our first lab." She added hopefully, "We'll be picking lab partners."

"Do you think anyone in class could act as my translator?"

She wanted to say something witty, but her head was always asleep when her heart was awake. "Nope."

"But you understand me?"

"Oh, I'm an exception." *Ask me! Ask me!*

"Would you be my lab partner?"

The day was definitely taking a turn for the better. She smiled. "Sure." Rick was over, done with, definitely.

Vanessa Barlow sat in the emptying stands of the gym, musing on how late she would be to fifth period and how little she cared. It was art II and Mr. Felix, who taught the class, was a wimp and wouldn't dare write her up as late. He would be afraid she might speak to her father — Frederick Barlow, superintendent of schools. Tarenton High had laid off more than one teacher recently.

"Coming, Van?" Steve Dextrile, school quarterback and her current boyfriend, asked. Six-two and 180 pounds of conditioned grit, he would have been handsome if the doctors hadn't messed up repairing the broken nose he'd gotten last fall, running into a goal post. As it was, his crooked nose matched the off-center squint of his eyes and mind. She supposed she liked him well enough. He kept her amused. Their demands on each other's company were easy to satisfy and didn't involve a lot of elaborate conversation.

"No. I'm staying here," Vanessa said.

"You'll be late to class."

"So?"

"Should I go on ahead?" He was waiting with a few of his buddies. She smiled for their benefit.

"Yeah. I'll see you after sixth. Give me a ride home?"

"No problem," he nodded, walking away with his pals. She had him well trained.

Vanessa did not want to go to fifth period because she had a lot on her mind. The pep rally had brought much of what had been troubling her all summer into focus, reawakening the bitterness she felt over not having made the Varsity Cheerleading Squad last spring. Not a single one of the girls, with the possible exception of Mary Ellen, was as good as she was. Oh, sure, the others — Nancy, Olivia, and Angie — could jump and shout. But they weren't as pretty as she was, and what did the guys on the team want cheerleaders for if not to look at them?

That's finished and done with, she thought. What am I going to do now?

A second goal loomed on the horizon, one more tantalizing than simply being a cheerleader. In a few weeks, Tareton High's student body would elect their homecoming queen. She wanted to be that queen. She knew she deserved to be. Yet she also knew if the election were held today, she would finish a distant second to Mary Ellen. Mary Ellen had long legs and hair, and her ivory skin was as clear as her blue eyes. Her own hair was probably shinier, though dark, and her complexion appeared equally flawless if she took the time with her make-up. The guys always went for a full figure and that was one area where she had an unquestionable edge. When it came to the bottom line, they were evenly matched. But Mary Ellen would still beat her, for Mary Ellen was extremely popular.

Vanessa's disadvantage was two-fold. Not only was her rival well liked, Vanessa Barlow had made too many enemies in her years at Tarenton High. Well, she had no regrets. You couldn't please everybody. On the other hand, for the next few weeks it might be to her advantage to do just that. People were fickle — one sweet word to them and they forget years of animosity. Her "witch" image could be easily erased with the right propaganda. Also, Mary Ellen's "sweetheart" image could just as easily be wiped out. Vanessa began to smile. The plans were coming together. This was going to be fun.

Her mother was an active member of UNICEF (United Nations International Children's Emergency Fund). She gave talks to PTAs, solicited donations from local businesses, did mailings of pamphlets with colored pictures of hungry children. The community applauded her humanitarianism. Vanessa got tired of listening to her. But wouldn't it please her mom no end if Vanessa took an interest in world hunger? Wouldn't it be possible to start a club on campus to make the local kids aware of the problem and raise money for starving children? Wouldn't it only be proper if she made herself president of the club and took all the credit? Wouldn't that make all prospective voters of the new homecoming queen think that she was one big-hearted young woman?

Would it? Vanessa wondered cautiously. Starting and running a club required a lot of work, never mind the red tape that would have to be cut through. It was very possible she would get absolutely no response. Still, it was something to consider.

The other half of the problem, the destruction of Mary Ellen's image, would require a more elaborate plan. First and foremost, she had to get her off the cheerleading squad. Getting to dance in front of everyone at the pep rallies and football games twice a week gave her too much of an advantage. Half the freshmen boys must already be in love with her. What she had to do was set Mary Ellen up somehow. . . .

Maybe a party! She could throw it next week at her house after the game. Her parents would be going away that weekend and the game was early on Saturday. She would invite everybody. The party would generate a heap of goodwill toward her by giving everyone a good time, and she would have a chance to corner Mary Ellen. The details of exactly what she would do to her weren't clear yet, but. . . .

She would think of something.

CHAPTER

A cloud of dust chased the red Porsche as Preston Tilford III swung off the asphalt highway onto Nature Lane, which had earned its name by being nothing more than a dirt path strewn with pebbles. Pres hated to subject the car, which had been a birthday present, to such a rough road but he couldn't very well drop Walt Manners off a mile from his home, since he *had* offered to drive Walt home from school.

"What is it like living way out here away from civilization?" Pres asked, downshifting to third, drooping trees momentarily enclosing them like walls of a cave.

"Quiet."

"Does it ever get to you?"

"Sometimes." Walt smiled. "But then I just go outside and holler for a few minutes."

"I bet the animals love that."

"They're used to me. They holler back." Walt

sat back, resting a knee on the glove compartment, his eyes half closed in his full face, his thick, dark hair blowing in the breeze from the open window. "I sure appreciate this ride. My jeep should be out of the shop by tomorrow."

"It's okay. I couldn't find you in the confusion after the pep rally. How did you like it?"

"I had a great time."

"So did I." He *had* enjoyed himself, and for some reason, that made him feel guilty. Probably he still hadn't adjusted to the idea of being a cheerleader. Certainly his parents hadn't. "Engborg stopped me afterwards, complimented us on a good job. Though I don't think she was wild about Mary Ellen's speech."

"Mary Ellen showed a lot of energy," Walt said emphatically. "She was great."

Oh no, Pres thought, here it comes again. He should have known better than to bring up Mary Ellen around Walt. Lately, the guy was obsessed with her. It had started suddenly. Pres hated to see him chasing a no-win situation. Once in private he had asked Mary Ellen if she found Walt attractive. Her laugh had said it all. Walt appeared all fun and games, but Pres knew he could be hurt. He had come to know him pretty well since they had made the squad last spring, well enough to recognize his two distinct sides: The Clown and The Romanticist.

"I think Mary Ellen's dazzling," Walt went on. "She's definitely the most attractive girl in the school."

Pres grunted noncommittally. Another reason he disliked discussing Mary Ellen with Walt was because he was beginning to take an interest in her himself, though he hadn't let Mary Ellen know yet. Last year he had dismissed her as a simple opportunist who used her beauty to get what she wanted, and he'd just joked around with her. He had since revised that evaluation. She was anything but simple. For example, the way she had hosted the pep rally today showed she knew how to control and inspire a crowd — not an easy task. Now whether she was an opportunist or not had yet to be determined by him. He had seen hints that indicated she wasn't opposed to trampling a few toes to get her way. But she was so incredible-looking, it was easy to overlook her faults. Before he had learned of Walt's obsession, he had made up his mind to ask her out. Now he hated to stab the guy in the back.

"I love the way she wears those red and white ribbons in her hair," Walt said. "They highlight her blue eyes."

Pres nodded, seeing no purpose in pointing out that *all* the girls in the squad often wore red and white ribbons in their hair. Pres could *feel* the question coming.

"Do you think I should ask her out?" Walt asked.

"Didn't you ask her out last year?" Pres said vaguely, knowing that Walt had, with no luck.

"That was different. She didn't know me well, then. Now we're good friends."

"Isn't she seeing Patrick Henley?"

Walt waved his hand indifferently. "Angie said Mary Ellen just dates him once in a while."

Angie was a reliable source of information. She

didn't clutter the facts with her own prejudices. Pres took it as good news. Then he quickly remembered that it was Walt who was in love with her. He asked his next question reluctantly. "Have you ever asked Angie if Mary Ellen has given her any idea of what she thinks of you?"

"No. Why should I?"

"So you would know, of course," Pres answered.

"Why don't I ask Mary Ellen herself?"

Because she might laugh in your face, Pres thought. "I don't think now is the time to ask her out," he mumbled.

"Why not?"

"Well . . . your jeep is in the shop and —"

"It'll be fixed tomorrow."

"And you mentioned that you were low on money."

"I can always borrow money from my parents," Walt laughed. "Hey, are you sure *you* don't have a crush on her?"

"I confess, I fantasize about her every night," he laughed, thinking he could get away with the exaggerated truth rather than an outright lie. It seemed to work. Walt turned away, chuckling as he tried to snatch leaves from the branches that brushed lightly against the car, all signs of suspicion gone — if there had been any to begin with.

"I think I'll ask her to Vanessa's party," Walt said.

"Vanessa's having a party? I didn't hear anything about it," Pres said.

"I have Vanessa in fifth period — art. She

came in late today, started talking about all the preparations she was making. It's going to be after next week's game."

"But Mary Ellen hates Vanessa. There's no way she would go with you."

Walt shrugged. He didn't understand one person hating another, because he didn't hate anybody . . . yet. "It's a party. What does it matter who's giving it? If I ask Mary Ellen, she'll go."

From that point on, the topic seemed closed. It was just as well. A minute more and they were at Walt's ultramodern log cabin that his parents had built. The house was a trip. There was a room outfitted as a video recording studio where they'd let Pres film a three-minute documentary on the tragedies of his life: when his dog had died, when his father had told him he would one day have to run the family business, when he had told his father to go jump in the lake. The documentary hadn't been one hundred percent accurate, but it had caught the essence of his life.

Walt asked him in for a Coke but Pres declined. He was anxious to get over to Winston, a neighboring city, to pick up a part for a machine in his dad's plant. So far he had managed to avoid working in the factory proper, but he was often used as an errand boy. This was his father's not-so-subtle way of trying to interfere with his cheerleading practice. His father believed that guys who were cheerleaders in high school eventually turned out like Boy George.

He said good-bye to Walt and spun back onto Nature Lane. Reaching the highway, he shifted into fifth, and began to open up the throttle. As he headed west, he was driving into the glare of the sun. It was therefore no surprise that he was a hundred yards past Mary Ellen before he realized who it was standing in the road. He hit the brake hard.

Mary Ellen cursed and kicked the wheel of her bike. It was flat, the stupid blasted thing! Now it would take her forever to get home.

"And it's so hot," she groaned, wiping the sweat from her brow with her already damp sleeve. She was still in her cheerleader uniform, and dreaded getting it stained. What a mess. If only she had a car and could drive like a normal person. If only she had a boyfriend who didn't want to drive her home in a garbage truck. If only. . . .

"I hadn't been born!" she shouted at a passing car. It wasn't listening, whipping by at twenty miles over the speed limit, throwing a cloud of dust in her eyes. Apparently she didn't look enough like a maiden in distress. Supporting the front wheel of her crippled bike and groaning again, she began to walk in the direction of her house in the old section of Tarenton.

But her day hadn't been so bad. Her impromptu speech at the pep rally, in spite of the fact that Mrs. Engborg had thought it was "flaky," had gone over well with the crowd. She smiled at the memory of the feeling of power she'd had, having the audience applaud when she wanted, laugh when she laughed. She must have that certain something after all, that indefinable charisma they would be looking for in New York in a prospective model. And who could tell — maybe modeling would only be a stepping stone to a stage career . . . a life on the big screen. The fantasy unrolled vividly before her, making the road seem not so long. She would have to shorten her name. Maybe she could just become M.E.

When the red Porsche slammed on its brakes, Mary Ellen's heart flew into her mouth. She had become so absorbed in her daydreaming that she hadn't realized that a car was passing. When it backed up alongside her and the driver leaned out the window, however, she recovered her bearing instantly.

"Going my way?"

"Pres! You scared me. Do you always drive so fast?"

"Only when the sun's in my eyes." He pulled to the side of the road and parked. "Did you run over glass?" He turned off the engine and climbed out.

She was glad to see him. He had changed out of his cheerleading uniform into tight blue jeans and an equally tight red shirt that granted generous glimpses of his deeply tanned chest. His eyes were dark, contrasting his blond hair with strangely complimentary results. Pres knew he was a fox, but that was okay. The arrogance was attractive in him.

Yet it was humiliating to be found in such a low life predicament. All week she had gone out of her way to create the illusion among the other squad members that she had a ride home. After practice each day, when no one was watching, she had slipped away to the far side of campus where she had her bike locked. It was inevitable the others would find out, but why did it have to be today, and why did Pres have to be the one?

She smiled brightly. "All I know is, I was cruising along and suddenly the ground got awfully bumpy."

Pres knelt, examining the tire, taking five seconds to find a tack, holding it up for her to see. "Looks like this is the culprit."

"Just my luck, it's probably the only tack on the road."

Pres took a seat on the curb. "Do you pedal home every day?"

"Oh, no! Just today. I didn't have a ride."

"Do you have a car?"

There was no sense lying. "No, but I can usually get a ride with my mom . . . friends . . . you know. I have a driver's license."

Pres must have recognized her embarrassment. He didn't try to pin her down. "Obviously your bike won't fit in my car, but I have a blanket and some rope in the trunk. I could tie it on the back and give you a ride home."

She didn't want him to see the ugly house she called home. Pres's parents owned the biggest — in fact, the only — mansion in Tarenton. "Don't bother, you might scratch your car. I don't have that far to go."

"I know where you live," he said, to her surprise. "That's a mile-and-a-half from here. It'll take you a while to get that far pushing that bike in this heat. Don't worry about my car. The blanket will protect the paint." He paused, looking away, as if he were suddenly unsure of himself. The transformation was as noticeable as it was abrupt. He added quietly, "Actually, I've got to drive to Winston to pick up a piece of equipment. I'd like some company. Would you like to come?"

The blood flow in her body accelerated, warming her already hot face and making her heart pound. This was ridiculous! She saw Pres every day! But then, it wasn't every day he asked her to join him in anything. This was just what she wanted. "Sounds like fun."

He stood up, smiling. "Great. I'll get the rope. We could stop for a Coke on the way back." He unlocked the trunk and pulled out a thick green blanket.

"I'm in no hurry to get home," she reassured him. It had been a good day so far and it looked like the best was still to come.

CHAPTER

Cool darkness surrounded her the next day, as Olivia Evans entered the gym to practice before first period, enjoying the time to focus that the solitude allowed. She didn't need the extra practice to be as good as the other girls — she simply wanted to be better than they. It was her nature to want to excel. Only in the gym could she get a genuine workout. When she practiced at home, her mother always watched with one hand on the phone, half the numbers to the paramedics already dialed. Her mom couldn't get rid of the memory of her blue-tinged, gasping daughter. The last heart operation had been years before and the doctors had long ago given her a clean bill of health, but to her mother, she was still a sick child. The main reason Olivia had gone out for the squad was to have an excuse to be away from home a few extra hours each day.

She was finishing her warm-up when she noticed the black-haired head peeking in through the door. How long he had been standing there, she had no idea.

"Can I help you?" she asked hesitantly. She wasn't very good at talking to boys. They frightened her. He pushed the door open and stepped inside. He was thin and sinewy, his high cheek bones and large black eyes striking even from a distance. She recognized him from last year, but couldn't place his name.

"I wanted a drink of water," he said, breathing heavily, walking slowly in her direction. He wore white shorts and a white T-shirt with *Tarenton Cross-Country* stenciled across the front in red. She remembered having seen his picture in the local paper last spring. He had won the state mile competition.

"Mrs. Engborg said it was okay if I practiced in here," she said quickly. Actually, Mrs. Engborg's permission had not been for this early an hour.

"Fine with me. Practice all you want." He detoured past her to the drinking fountain. She decided she should at least try to make conversation.

"Are you on the cross-country team?"

He nodded, gulping the water thirstily.

"That's nice . . . I'm a cheerleader."

He straightened, glanced her way. "I know."

"Of course, you must have seen me at the pep rally."

"I never go to pep rallies."

Didn't everyone go to pep rallies? "Were you at the game Friday?"

"No. I hate football."

So do I, Olivia thought. But she couldn't say that and still be a pinnacle of school spirit. She forced a smile. "We won, forty-nine to seven."

"So did the cross-country team." There was an edge in his voice, as though he might be angry or disappointed. He took another drink and wiped at his mouth.

"Who did you play, I mean run against?"

"Excelsior, the same school the football team played."

"Did you win by a lot?"

"We took the first five places."

"That's good. How did you do, personally?"

"Good." He glanced around the empty gym. "I should probably leave . . . let you practice."

Olivia didn't want him to go. He was . . . interesting. There was an intensity in his eyes, a strength in his face. She took a gamble. "Did you win the race?"

He shrugged. "Yeah, but it was no big deal."

"Sure it was." Listen to her — she sounded as confident as Mary Ellen. "Were many people there?"

"A few. Our races don't get much publicity. Look, I've got to run another three miles before first period. Nice talking to you." He jogged toward the door.

"When is your next race?" she called. Afterwards, she was sure, she wouldn't believe she had been so assertive.

He stopped. "Why?"

"I was thinking that I could talk to some of the girls on the squad and we could come to the race."

"Forget it. Cross-country meets are boring."

Olivia was taken aback. "You don't want us to come?"

He was edging for the door. "You can come if you want. All I'm saying is that there isn't too much excitement. It's Friday at three-thirty."

"Then why do you do it if it isn't exciting?" she asked as much out of frustration as anything else. This was the first talk she'd had alone with a boy in a long time, and it wasn't going well. Probably he just found her unexciting and couldn't wait to get away. He pulled open the door.

"That's a long story."

"But . . . ?"

"Don't bother yourself, Olivia," he called, disappearing.

"But I have time," she whispered to no one. He was a most unusual guy. She did not believe he had said what was on his mind. Maybe the cheerleading squad had snubbed the cross-country team last year and he was resentful. She would have to check that out, talk to Mary Ellen. She would also find out where the next meet would be. She would go, even if what's his name didn't want her there.

Suddenly, Olivia remembered his name — Michael Barnes.

Interesting how he had known *her* name.

"See any?" Nancy asked Alex as she returned from a brief trip to the restroom, taking a seat at their lab table at the rear of Creol's biology class. A microscope and an assortment of slides stained with amoeba-saturated water covered the grey formica counter.

"Nope," he muttered, squinting through the eyepiece. "Is this really an amoeba solution? I'd swear that the teach just poured green dye in this goop."

"Wouldn't that be ironic," she said, already celebrating the fact that Alex was her lab partner. His natural wit would keep her entertained the rest of the year. But though he was nice to her, she didn't know if he liked her, or rather, she didn't know if he liked *her* in particular. He was nice to everybody!

"I wonder," he said, sitting back from the instrument, "if Mr. Creol could simply be testing us." He nodded to himself. "In fact, I'm sure that's what he's doing. I've looked and looked — there's no amoeba in this water."

Was he serious? She didn't know him well enough to know when he was pulling her leg. "Let's keep looking. If we find one we'll be sure."

He shook his head, leaning close, lowering his voice. "There's a better way. Amoebas have a distinct flavor."

She chuckled. "Get out of here. I'm sure not going to drink . . . *Alex*!"

He had picked up the beaker holding the sample, and raised it to his lips. "A small taste ought to tell me one way or the other," he said, checking to make sure no one else was watching. Before she could stop him, he took a sip. "Boy, this is awful," he frowned. "I'm still not sure."

"Alex!" He could get sick — if he wasn't already sick, in the head! I knew he was too good to be true, she thought, frantically trying to get the beaker from his hand. He held it out of reach.

"Calm down, Nancy. This is a scientific experiment. I have to be sure." And with that he tilted the beaker to his mouth and drained it to the last drop. Nancy stared at him, speechless, expecting him to black out. He wiped at his lips, apparently refreshed. "There were definitely amoebas in that water."

Nancy clutched at her stomach. "I'm going to be sick." But before her nausea could take hold, Alex began to laugh. She knew the truth in an instant — she'd been had. "What was it!?" she glared.

"Lime soda!" He gasped. "I got it from my locker when you went to the restroom!"

He hadn't pulled her leg, he had amputated it at the hip. "*You*!" she pushed him and he laughed all the harder.

"This is a scientific experiment!" he said.

She went to kick him, but a stern voice stopped her foot in midair.

"Quiet down back there!" Mr. Creol called. Looking up, Nancy was surprised to find Vanessa Barlow, arms laden with pamphlets and a thick notebook, standing next to their wrinkled and stooped biology teacher. Nancy had not seen her come in. Wearing a short sleeved purple dress and a yellow ribbon in her black hair, Vanessa looked good. But then, Nancy thought, so did junk wrapped in gift paper.

"Everyone, please stop what you are doing," Mr. Creol continued. "Right now, we have a special guest speaker. Ordinarily, I wouldn't allow an interruption to our routine, but this young lady has come to tell you about a cause that all of you should give some thought to joining. May I introduce Vanessa Barlow."

What could Vanessa possibly be connected with that wasn't designed to spread grief, Nancy wondered?

"I would like to thank Mr. Creol for giving me a chance to speak," Vanessa began, surveying the room briefly to make sure she had everyone's attention. "Basically, I'm here to make you aware of a new club forming on campus, called 'Food for the Forgotten.' Its purpose is to raise money for food to send to starving people in third world countries. The club is open to all students regardless of grade. Our first scheduled meeting is this Friday at lunch in room GS 84."

Vanessa paused to hop up on the counter behind which Mr. Creol usually lectured, swinging her legs easily. "Without wanting to sound preachy, there are a lot of hungry people in the world . . . millions, in fact. Tens of thousands of these people die each year from malnutrition. Imagine what it would be like to go day after day with no sure knowledge of when you would eat again? Obviously, it would be horrible, and yet there are continents full of people where that has become the norm. And the sad part is they require so little support to have their lives drastically improved. If I may, I would like to quote some figures."

Vanessa consulted her notebook and read off how far five dollars a month could go to save a hungry child. The class listened closely. Nancy had to admit that she had done her homework. At the close of her speech, she passed out pamphlets, postponing all questions until the first meeting.

"Remember, you don't have to join the club to support its aims," she added, getting down from the counter. "The club will be establishing an account at a bank in town to accept contributions. Every penny will be used to buy food." She closed her notebook. "Thanks again for your time."

Their teacher shook her hand. "Thank you, Vanessa. It's wonderful to see students' interests include more than what clothes they should wear and how popular they are."

Vanessa blushed and, collecting her materials, turned to leave. At the door, however, she stopped, adding, "If for any reason you are unable to come to the meeting Friday, talk to me Saturday evening after the game at my house," she laughed. "I'm having a big party where I guarantee none of you will starve!"

With Vanessa gone, Mr. Creol ordered them back to their microscopes. Slipping in another slide, Alex said, "I'm going to try to make that meeting. Vanessa sounds like a sharp girl. I hope her club accomplishes a lot of good."

Nancy wanted to explain that Vanessa's history was far from illustrious, but she was afraid it would come out sounding like sour grapes. "I hope so," she muttered.

Alex began to giggle again. "I was impressing you with my unusual tastes."

She scowled. "If it takes me all year, I'm going

to make you pay for that one." Then she smiled. "It *was* pretty funny. Have you ever thought of being a comedian?"

"I'm already in the entertainment business." He pointed to his earring. "I suppose you've noticed this?"

"Well . . . now that you mention it."

He tugged on it lightly. "Does it make you uncomfortable?"

"No! Not at all."

"It's part of my look." Now he was being serious. "I see jewelry as an extension of my personality. I feel different, so I want to look different."

"Even if it might make some people . . . uncomfortable?"

"That doesn't bother me. My self-image is not dependent on what others think or say about me. I couldn't live that way."

"I wish I felt that way." It sure would make life a lot simpler. Her whole life revolved around how others saw her.

"Anyway, to be less philosophical," he went on, "I'm in a band. You've seen enough videos on MTV to know musicians like to dress weird."

"You've only been in Tarenton a couple of months. How did you get in a band so quick?"

He smiled. "I went into a music store in Winston and saw an ad up on the board describing a new wave group looking for a singer. I gave them a call, they gave me an audition, and we all got together. I also play the piano."

"I'm impressed."

"Shouldn't you wait to hear us play before you say that?"

Was he asking her out? She wasn't sure, and all of a sudden her stomach didn't feel so hot. "I'd like that . . . to hear you play, that is," she stuttered.

"Great. We're opening at the Clinton a week from Saturday. I'd love to have you there."

Far out, she thought. Then she felt even more nervous. It seemed you couldn't be happy without having an equal amount of misery. "What's the . . . Clinton?"

"It's a club in Winston. They ask for ID at the door, but it's no problem. I can get you in the back."

It *was* a problem. Her parents wouldn't let her have the car to drive to Winston. That meant Alex would have to take her — he probably had that in mind — and that meant he would have to meet her parents. Her father had never adjusted to her going out with boys. Imagine how he'd feel about her dating a boy who wore a gold earring in his right ear. She doubted seriously that her parents would let Alex in the house. Her dad was a nice man and she loved him. It was just that he insisted she do what was *right*, and had ideas in that regard that were vastly different from her own.

There were other complications. As a cheerleader, she was forbidden alcohol. It was one of Mrs. Engborg's commandments. Even if she didn't drink at the club, simply being seen there would be enough to have her expelled from the squad. And it was very possible somebody from school — it would only take one gossiper — would be there that Saturday night, required ID notwithstanding. Above all else, she couldn't be dropped from the squad.

"That sounds like fun," she said after only a moment's hesitation. "Ahh . . . do you play late?"

"No, to one o'clock or so."

That was late. She wouldn't get back home till two. Her father would be waiting on the front porch with the clock. "I'll be looking forward to it," she smiled. Good grief!

CHAPTER

She's going to steal the money for the starving children and spend it on clothes, Mary Ellen thought, watching Vanessa Barlow leaving Mr. Chambers' sixth period English class.

"She was very inspiring," Walt said, sitting in the seat behind her. Mary Ellen turned and faced him. Good old Walt, not a corrupt bone in his body. He didn't know when he was being conned.

"She made me want to weep," Mary Ellen said sarcastically.

He chuckled. "You don't like Vanessa very much, do you?"

"It's not that I don't like her — I *hate* her."

His sudden look of concern surprised her. "But you *do* want to go to her party, don't you?"

It was her turn to laugh. "I'd rather go to a funeral. Can't you see what Vanessa's up to?" She checked to make sure she was not attracting attention. Mr. Chambers ran his class unlike any other teacher at Tarenton High. All they had to do was read one book every two weeks and write about it in a notebook they handed in. Besides serving as a book report medium, the notebook was used, at Mr. Chambers' encouraging, to put down whatever was on their minds. This gave them a means to sort out for themselves what was on their minds. He wasn't playing the role of a psychotherapist. Once a problem was down on paper, it usually didn't appear so fearsome. The key was knowing they had a perfect confidant in Mr. Chambers, even if he never actually told them what to do.

"She's just launching a large scale image-improvement program," Mary Ellen continued. "Vanessa doesn't care about starving children in Africa. She can't even be bothered feeding her dog."

"Isn't she going to a lot of trouble simply to improve her image?" Walt asked.

"She has a strong motive. She wants to be homecoming queen. Next week the five princesses will be selected. Two weeks after that one of those five will be elected queen. Vanessa's already on the campaign trail."

"That's wild," Walt laughed. "She must know she doesn't stand a chance against you."

Mary Ellen smiled. "Thanks, that's sweet. But I wouldn't be so sure. She *is* awfully pretty." The reason Mary Ellen understood Vanessa so well was because *she* wanted to be homecoming queen just as much. If she were queen, there wouldn't be a guy in school she couldn't have. Even Preston Tilford III.

"So I can't talk you into going to the party with me?" Walt's voice interrupted her brief daydreaming.

"Hmm?"

"You definitely don't want to go to the party?"

"No, I think I'll stay home and read *The Encyclopedia Britannica.*"

"Will you be going out with Patrick that night?" Walt asked.

The mention of Patrick's name brought its usual discomfort. Sunday morning, for the umpteenth time, she had decided she wasn't going to see him again. Then he had called that afternoon and asked her to go to the movies. Why had she given in? Probably out of boredom, along with a generous helping of insecurity. And once again being near him had made her want to hold him and be kissed by him — to let him love her totally. With Pat she knew where she stood. Not so with Pres. One way or the other, this would have to be resolved, at least in her own mind. Perhaps writing it down would help. It had in the past.They should probably quiet down now anyway. Mr. Chambers didn't mind talking, but that didn't go for all the students in class.

"Excuse me, Walt," she whispered, touching his arm, "can we talk after class?"

"Sure."

Mary Ellen spun back to her desk top and notebook, pulled the cap off her pen, and wrote to Mr. Chambers:

I'd like your advice on a problem I have. I've told you about Patrick Henley, and what I feel for him. But I haven't told you the reservations I have about seeing him now that school is back in session. I'm shallow, a phony, I know. But I can't stop thinking that everyone is laughing at me behind my back for dating a garbage man. To complicate matters, there's another boy I do want to be with — for shallow, phony reasons. He's one of the boys on our squad — that should tell you his name. I've known him awhile. We just never "made contact" until last Thursday.

Mary Ellen set down her pen and thought back to what happened the day before, after Pres tied her bike to the rear of his Porsche. First, he rolled up the windows and put on the air-conditioning and she was able to cool off. The smell of the leather seats was delicious. She had never been in a car that cost as much as a Porsche did. While they sped toward Winston, he told her about his ongoing conflict with his father and how he had initially gone out for the squad just to irritate him. She liked his openness. During camp and practice they had discussed nothing but their routines. She responded by telling him of her dream of becoming a New York model. She didn't dwell on her family's money situation. He might think she was on the prowl for a rich boyfriend . . . and he would be right.

At Winston they picked up the part for his father's factory and stopped at a nearby ice-cream parlor for a malt. He didn't seem surprised when she borrowed a dime to call home. Asking for the ten cents was embarrassing, but it was the lesser of two evils. As it was, her mother was already worrying where she was.

He drove much slower on the way back. She took that as a sign that he was enjoying her company. Yet he spoke less, and appeared troubled, into his own thoughts. When we finally dropped her off, she was ashamed to invite him in, and he didn't say anything about them dating. But Pres did reach for her and kiss her. Mary Ellen summoned all her acting ability to pretend she felt the excitement that Pres was feeling, but all she felt was pleasure that he wanted her. Her thoughts drifted to Patrick, to *his* mouth and hands and arms. If it was Patrick kissing her now. . . .

At the game the next night, the distance between them was the same as it had been before.

What was the problem?

Grabbing her pen, she returned to her journal.

In fact, Pres has the things that Pat lacks. He has social position, money, and a beautiful house, and clean fingernails. You'd think my choice would be easy. It isn't. I know Pres doesn't really care for me. He finds me interesting, but I think it would take a miracle to find someone who loves me as much as Patrick does. This is what confuses me the most. I don't want to hurt Patrick. In a crazy way, despite his being broke, he's made my life rich.

What should I do?

The bell rang. Mary Ellen quickly reread what she had written, tore out the page and ripped it into pieces. She trusted Mr. Chambers but if this were to accidentally fall into the wrong hands. . . .

Anyway, she knew what he was going to say: *You have to make up your own mind, Mary Ellen.*

Walt followed her out into the courtyard. Cheerleading practice was next. They usually walked over to the locker rooms together. "What did you want to ask me?" she said casually.

"I wanted . . . I wanted to ask you —"

"Mary Ellen!"

It was Olivia, who seldom talked to her outside of practice. She watched as the small, lithe girl hurried through the criss-crossing bodies to reach her side.

"Coming to practice with us, Olivia?" she asked.

"I never miss practice," Olivia said seriously. "I want to talk to you."

"Let's talk while we walk." She wanted to get a lot accomplished in practice. The state cheerleading preliminaries were in two weeks and they weren't anywhere near ready for intense competition. They needed . . . more fireworks . . . something, she wasn't quite sure what.

"How many cross-country meets did you go to last year?" Olivia asked.

"None," she said.

Olivia was shocked. "You didn't go to a single one?"

"I did," Walt said, "But they wouldn't let me run so I left."

"No one goes to cross-country meets," Mary Ellen explained. "Who wants to watch a herd of skinny boys run around a field?"

"I wouldn't mind watching a herd of skinny girls," Walt said.

Olivia thought about that for a minute. Mary Ellen wondered if she had met a guy on the CC team, then dismissed the idea. Olivia didn't talk to boys. Her mother must have convinced her that boys were bad for her heart.

"Did you know that last year Tarenton High's cross-country team won the league championship?" Olivia said finally.

"No," Mary Ellen said. "It sounds like they're doing fine without us."

"But it is our responsibility to support *all* our athletic teams," Olivia said carefully. "This Friday, they'll be having a meet starting at three-thirty."

"We have practice then," Mary Ellen said. She had nothing against the runners, it was just that there was no fame in attending their meets.

"We could stop a half hour early and still make the first race," Olivia said reasonably. "The starting and finishing points are in the stadium. It would take us five minutes to walk there from the gym."

What Olivia was asking was no big deal. However, Olivia didn't have to spend half an hour pedaling home. Mary Ellen had no idea how long the meets lasted, but *nothing* took less than an hour and *nothing* started earlier than a half hour late. It was getting dark earlier . . . maybe a compromise would work. I'll probably need the CC team's votes to beat Vanessa, Mary Ellen thought.

"I'll make a deal with you. We'll quit practice early, and those who want to go to the meet can. I can't, but I'll see if I can't make room for Coach Riley to speak at this week's pep rally where he can introduce his varsity runners. All this, of course, is dependent on Mrs. Engborg's approval."

CHAPTER

The first Food for the Forgotten meeting was held Friday and had gone well. Judging from the number of questions and the level of enthusiasm, Vanessa wouldn't be surprised to see most of them become full-fledged members. Fortunately, no one had asked exactly what they were going to do. She still had to think that one out. Her mother, in seventh heaven over her "conscientious daughter," would have some ideas. All was going well. The club had already nominated Vanessa president.

"I never knew you were such an excellent public speaker," Cathleen Eismar said. The two of them were alone in the meeting room, the doors shut. Cathleen was a recent addition to her fan club. One of the Eismar twins, who also didn't make the squad; she felt her friendship with Vanessa separated her from her twin, Shelley. But what made Cathleen such a potentially valuable pal was that up until last spring she had been casual friends with both Mary Ellen and Nancy Goldstein. Then she had been eliminated as a candidate for the squad and had become envious of them. Vanessa had not been surprised that the girl had been passed over. Cathleen would have made a dreadful cheerleader.

"What's this I hear about Mary Ellen not coming to my party tomorrow night?" Vanessa asked. She had thought she had covered that possibility by speaking to Patrick Henley earlier in the week. He had promised he would bring Mary Ellen.

"Patrick called in sick today with the flu. He'll probably still be sick tomorrow. But even if Mary Ellen had a date, she wouldn't come. We have English together and I heard her telling Walt Manners she'd rather attend a funeral."

"There must be some way of getting her there."

"Vanessa, *why* do you want that stuck-up jerk at your party?"

"She's going to be the entertainment."

"What do you mean?"

"You'll see. If we get her to the party, she'll make a bigger fool out of herself than she tried to make out of *us* last spring." She paused to let the reminder sink in. "You mentioned once that your little sister, Clara, was a friend of Mary Ellen's sister, Gemma."

"You've lost me."

The girl was dense. "I want you to approach Mary Ellen tomorrow at the game and tell her that you have a present for Gemma from Clara that you'll give her at the party."

"Why don't I just give it to her at the game?"

"Because you don't have it with you. But you *will* have it at the party. Come on, there must be something your sister would like to give to her good friend?"

Cathleen thought for a minute. "Clara did mention a new pair of jeans that are tight on her that would probably fit Gemma better."

"Perfect."

"What if Mary Ellen wants to pick them up another time?"

"Act insulted. Act as if now that she's a cheerleader, she doesn't have time for you."

Cathleen was bitter. "She *doesn't* have time for me."

"Then you don't have to act. Also, give the impression that it is a surprise present. In fact, wrap up the jeans in gift paper. Mary Ellen's self-centered, but when it comes to her sister, she does an about-face. She'll stop by."

"How are you going to keep her there?" Cathleen asked.

"Leave that to me."

"But *what* are you going to do to her?"

Vanessa smiled. "I'm going to put her in my debt, that's all."

At three o'clock, Olivia trailed behind Walt, Angie, and Nancy as they walked up the ramp that led to the stadium. It was *hot,* like it had been every day since school had begun. How could anyone run three miles in this oven? They should cancel the race, let the runners rest . . . let her not have to face Michael Barnes again.

"What time is it?" Olivia asked.

"A minute later than last time you asked," Angie laughed. "What's the matter with you today, Olivia?"

Olivia wiped her forehead. "I just don't want to be late."

Nancy fell by her side, whispering, "Is there someone on the CC team you're nervous about seeing?"

"I don't know any boys on the team."

"Okay," Nancy said quietly, "but if it's any comfort, I've got boy troubles of my own."

Walt and Angie began to pull away, passing inside the twenty-foot fence that rimmed the stadium grounds. Nancy stopped, shielding her eyes with her hands. "Where's that phone? I've got to call my mom and tell her not to pick me up at four. There it is, by the snack bar. I wish that thing was open. I could use a Coke."

"I should call my mother, too," Olivia said. She walked beside Nancy in silence, wanting to tell her about Michael, but afraid to expose her feelings, especially ones she did not understand. She had not spoken to Michael since Tuesday in the gym. She had seen him, of course, sitting alone with a book on the other side of the courtyard, but he had made no move toward her. He had not waved. She had not caught him staring in her direction. There was no reason to think he liked her . . . except that he had known her name. And that wasn't much to lose sleep over.

"Who is giving you trouble?" she asked tentatively.

"Alex. You met him," Nancy said. "He's asked

me out for a week from tomorrow."

Olivia wished she had Nancy's troubles. "Is that bad?"

"He's in a new wave band. He wants me to see him play in a club in Winston where they serve liquor, and where we'll be out all night. You saw the way he dresses. If he picked me up at home, who knows what my father would do."

"Ask Alex to dress like an ordinary guy when he comes to the house."

"I'm afraid to offend him. And that would only solve part of the problem. There is no way my father will let me stay out till two in the morning."

"Tell your parents that you are spending the night at my house and have Alex pick you up at school. The building's going to be open all day Saturday until at least nine. The seniors are rehearsing for their play." The suggestion was out of her mouth before she realized she'd spoken it.

"You mean *lie* to my parents?"

"No, I meant —"

"That's a great idea!"

"It is?"

Nancy looked up to the blue sky. "It would be easy to make up an excuse to tell Alex to explain why I'll be at school. I could even leave home early in the evening with an overnight bag."

"Wait a second," Olivia said. "I was only joking. What if your mom calls my house and wants to talk to you? What if someone from school sees you? If Mrs. Engborg found out, she'd kick you off the squad. If your father found out, he'd . . . I don't know what he would do."

"He'd ground me till my twenty-first birthday,"

Nancy said gloomily, "but I guess those are the chances I'll have to take."

"Have Alex take you to a movie instead."

Nancy shook her head. "This will be his opening night." She touched her arm. "Will you help me?"

"I don't want to help you get into trouble." No wonder she had kept her mouth shut these last sixteen years. She opened it once and immediately her life got complicated.

"I don't *want* to lie to my folks," Nancy said, "but I *have* to go on this date."

Olivia could see how much it meant to her. Nancy had never asked for a favor before. As a matter of fact, no one had. "I'll help you."

"Thanks." Nancy hugged her quickly. "What I won't do for love!"

After Nancy called home, Olivia dialed her own number. She braced herself for a scene, and wasn't disappointed. She had scarcely begun to explain why she would be late when her mother interrupted.

"Isn't it enough that you have to cheer at the football game tomorrow night? Put Mrs. Engborg on the line. I want to speak to her."

"She's not here. Mrs. Engborg isn't making us do this."

Her mother simmered. "When can I pick you up?"

"Nancy's mother is taking me home. I'll be okay, really. Now I have to go."

"That's right, go ahead and hang up. It's only your mother, who's kept you alive all these years, that you're talking to."

Besides being obsessed with her daughter's health, her mother was a martyr. "I'm not hanging up, but the races are about to start. I'll see you later."

Putting down the phone, Olivia sighed. "We both better pray that your mother doesn't call mine the night you go out with Alex. It would be the end of the world."

A crowd of sixty were gathered, eighty percent of them either Tarenton High or Stanton High runners. Michael was right about one thing — they didn't draw big crowds. Olivia didn't see him and felt both disappointed and relieved.

"Where is he?" Nancy whispered.

"He's not here."

"You haven't even told me your guy's name," Nancy said.

"His name is Michael Barnes and he's not my guy. The only time I spoke to him, he sounded mad."

"Let me guess, he was mad that no cheerleaders come to the cross-country meets?"

"He didn't say so, but I think it was bothering him."

Nancy laughed. "At least I know now why we're here. Don't worry, he's probably off warming up. He'll show up."

"That's what I'm worried about," Olivia muttered.

Coach Riley came over, his half dozen stopwatches ticking loudly. "Thanks for coming, girls. We appreciate the support."

Nancy cut in. "Excuse me. Is Michael Barnes running today?"

"Yes, and he should win with no trouble. Stanton High has no one that can touch him. He won't be tested until we race Wickfield. The Warriors have a young man — David Clare — who's sensational. Mike likes to warm up alone. That's why you don't see him around."

"Is his mother here?" Nancy asked. Olivia wished that she would kindly drop the subject.

Coach Riley shook his head. "Both his parents were killed in a car accident when he was a freshman. He lives with an uncle."

"That can be rough," Angie said, for a moment, serious.

"What did you think of the coach's scoop on Michael?" Nancy asked.

"It was sad."

"Yeah, but it gave another reason why he might have sounded angry when he talked to you. He's probably put up a wall to keep from getting hurt again. It looks to me like you'll have to play the role of the pursuer."

"I can't do that!"

"Is that him coming through the gate? Go over and wish him good luck."

Olivia cringed. Maybe her heart hadn't totally healed from her operation — it felt like the stitches were coming undone. "Will you come with me?"

"No! *You're* the one who's in love with him," Nancy said.

Olivia was aghast. "I am not in *love* with him!"

"Then why are you so afraid?" Nancy took pity on her, and went on gently, "I know how you feel.

believe me. But sometimes you've just got to take a running start and jump."

Olivia knew Nancy was right. Swallowing the dry lump in her throat, she began to walk toward Michael. Her emotions were a mixture of terror and numbness. She supposed that she was in mild shock. It had been a lot easier speaking to him the first time, before she'd had time to think about him.

"Hello, Michael," she called, relieved to hear her vocal cords still working. He was standing close to but still apart from his teammates. He turned her way. A faint smile touched his lips.

"Hi, how are you?"

She had been hoping that he would have used her name. It would have given her confidence. "I'm okay. How are you?"

"Fine."

"I brought . . . we . . . some of the cheerleaders came to root for you."

He began to stretch, reaching for his toes. She was probably disrupting his concentration. "That was nice of you."

"Well, I don't want to bother you. I just wanted to, you know, say hello, and wish you good luck."

He stopped and stared at her. His black eyes were as large as she remembered — round, deep wells. New warmth entered his voice. "I appreciate that. I'll try to do my best."

She chuckled, out of tension. "Oh, I know you're going to win." And because she wanted to end on this good note, she added hastily, "I'll let you get back to your warm-up. Good-bye."

"Good-bye, Olivia."

He hadn't forgotten her name. Feeling a foot taller, she hurried back to Nancy. When she was safely at Nancy's side, she turned to see Michael jog back out the gate.

"What did he say?" Nancy asked, excited.

"Nothing — hello, how are you."

"Why are you smiling?"

"I'm not smiling."

"Yes, you are, and you never smile. Now you'll have to congratulate him after he wins."

"Do you think that's wise? I don't want to overdo it for one day."

"There is no way, Olivia, that *you* could overdo it."

"I saw you talking to Michael Barnes," Walt said to Olivia. "Where is that guy? I want to speak to him."

"Don't," Olivia said, already feeling protective. "He likes to be alone before a race."

Nancy and Olivia passed out refreshments while Angie and Walt walked to the starting line with the varsity teams. Michael jogged in the back gate and threw off his sweats. The others, Titans and Wolves alike, moved aside for him in obvious awe. Coach Riley settled everyone on the starting line. And they were off!

"Yeah, Michael!!!" Olivia screamed, then put her hand over her mouth, embarrassed. Then she figured *what the heck*, and screamed his name even louder.

Less than fifteen minutes later, while waiting nervously, Olivia caught sight of Michael again, coming up the ramp, no other runners in sight.

She knew nothing about distance running, but it was clear that he was someone exceptional. His feet hardly seemed to touch the ground. If it hadn't been for the ground passing so swiftly beneath him, she would have thought he was moving in slow motion, such was the effortless grace in his stride. His eyes were half closed, his breathing deep and strong. The spectators burst into loud applause as he crested the ramp, she along with them. He circled the track and hit the tape, his nearest competitor still not in sight. Nancy poked Olivia.

"Go congratulate him. Give him a big kiss."

"Shouldn't I wait until he has had a chance to cool off?"

"You'll lose the dramatic element if you wait." Nancy shoved her in the back. "Go!"

It was much easier this time. She caught up with him in the center of the field. He was still trying to catch his breath, bent over, sweat dripping from his jersey like rain.

"Are you okay?"

"I heard you cheering for me when I came up the ramp," he whispered to the ground. "It gave me a boost."

"Really?" she said. "I think you would have done well without us. Can I get you anything? A towel? A drink?"

He stood upright, taking a deep, ragged breath, wiping at his red face. "I could use a drink."

"I'll get it for you." She turned for the ice chest.

"Wait."

She stopped. "Yes?"

"I wanted to ask you something," he gasped, having to bend over again.

"Go ahead, I'm listening."

He took an eternity to get it out. "Isn't there a game tomorrow night?"

"Yes. Are you coming?"

"I hate football."

"Oh."

"But . . ." he coughed, "isn't there a party that night?"

"Yes, at Vanessa Barlow's house."

He nodded weakly. "I don't mind parties . . . occasionally. I'll be there."

Her mother was going to throw a fit. Who cared? "I'll be there, too. I'll look for you."

He plopped down on the grass in exhaustion, bowing his head. "Good."

CHAPTER

"All the way down the field, HEY!! All the way down the field, HEY!! All the way down the field, HEY!"

Backed by two thousand cheering fans, Mary Ellen's chant literally shook the stadium, reverberating off the packed bleachers into the glare of the tungsten lamps and the dim of the fading twilight beyond. She was in total control, and Pres had to admire her for it. The enthusiasm of the audience was feverish. Sixty seconds to go and Tarenton High would head to the lockers for the halftime break, leading by at least three points — quite an accomplishment against the Titans, who didn't have a guy on their defensive line that weighed under two hundred pounds. Steve Dextrile, Tarenton's quarterback, was only ten yards from putting another six points on the board. Pres felt good.

Suddenly the crowd gasped. Pres whirled.

Steve's pass had been intercepted, and the Titan who had the ball was staring at relatively open territory and a four-point Stanton High lead. Mary Ellen didn't realize this.

"All the way down the field, HEY!! All the way down the field, HEY!!"

Mary Ellen was inadvertently cheering for the other team.

The Titan defensive end crossed the goal line and threw his arms up in ecstasy. Steve Dextrile tore off his helmet and threw it toward the sidelines. Pres grabbed his megaphone and pointed it at Mary Ellen.

"Cut it!" he shouted.

Mary Ellen lost her shiny smile, glanced at Pres, then at the scoreboard and the playing field, and shook her head in disgust. Pres walked over and patted her on the back. She turned away from the home crowd, from which a few hoots could still be heard. "How long have I been making a fool of myself?" she whispered.

"It happened quickly. Don't worry about it."

"I feel like a jerk."

"Not half as much as Steve does." Pres wanted to console her, but was not sure how. "Would you like a hot dog?"

She nodded, smiling for his benefit. "A hot dog sounds good."

It was a warm night, and there was already a thirsty crowd at the snack bar. While looking for the shortest line, Pres bumped into Vanessa.

"Hi, Pressy," she murmured. She was wearing a loose maroon blouse and tight white pants. Brushing aside her shiny mane of black hair, she poked his stomach, an old habit of hers that left him unmoved. She was beautiful and he was attracted to her. Although he knew she was viscious, she always turned him on. He had taken her out a few times — he had dated practically every Tarenton girl at least once — but Vanessa had talked so much and so fast she had left him with a headache. He knew what she was going to ask.

"Are you coming to my party?"

He had been leaning toward not going, since Walt had told him that Mary Ellen had no intention of putting in an appearance. It was a peculiar reason to be basing his decision on, as he had been intentionally avoiding her since their drive to Winston. Pres was becoming illogical and that was a sure sign he was getting involved. Today he had finally rationalized that his loyalty to Walt had its limits. Walt was living in a fantasy world. Why deny himself for no reason? She was cute — looking better every day, in fact. Mary Ellen was the kind of girl any guy would want to be seen with.

"I'll see," Pres said vaguely.

"Mary Ellen will be there," Vanessa giggled slyly.

Pres was startled. "Are you sure?"

She tapped his chest. "Come see for yourself. Now I've got to go and get the food ready." She ran out the gate and was lost in the night crowd. Pres decided he would ask Mary Ellen outright just what was what.

Mary Ellen gratefully accepted the orange

juice that Gemma gave her. Her throat was dry and her head was hot. Gemma had been a dear to run over to the snack bar for the drink. It was a shame she couldn't invite her down onto the track and let her have a firsthand view of what it was like to stand with a microphone and shout at the crowd.

"You owe me fifty cents," Gemma laughed, tilting the purple hat she wore at least once a day — a gift from her wonderful older sister on her thirteenth birthday last month. Mary Ellen had chosen the present with care. The purple complemented Gemma's midnight hair, the color matching the scattered flecks in the depth of her dark eyes.

"I'll give it to you tomorrow," she promised. "Plus tax."

"And interest," Mary Ellen nodded gravely. Then they laughed together. "How did I look cheering for the other team when that guy intercepted the ball?" She had already swallowed the humiliation, but she needed reassurance.

"Funny. Was that guy on the other team a friend of yours?"

"We go way back. Where's the folks?"

"Dad's getting hot dogs and Mom's up in the back row."

Mary Ellen had to smile — their mother was notoriously shy. She squeezed Gemma's hands. "Tell both of them hello for me. . . . No, tell them I love them."

Gemma nodded happily. "I'll wave from the last row next time there's an interception at your back."

"Sounds like a deal. Thanks for the juice."

"Fifty cents plus tax!"

"Get out of here!" Mary Ellen laughed, feeling almost embarrassed at the wave of tenderness that washed over her as she watched Gemma hop up the steps and disappear into the crowd. Fortunately for her "tough" self-image, her tender feelings were quickly interrupted.

"O Exalted One," two muffled voices said, "we earnestly beg an audience."

She turned to find Walt and Angie with their megaphones over their heads. Nancy stood between them, not looking nearly so playful. "What's on your mind?" Mary Ellen asked.

"O Exalted One," Walt said, "we of small minds and pointed heads would like to make a small suggestion."

"We wanted to suggest you take a break from the microphone," Nancy said bluntly.

"What?" she asked defensively.

"The nectar of your words, O Exalted One," Walt murmured, "is suffering in the grossness of this environment."

"What?"

"You're getting hoarse," Nancy said simply.

"I am not. Am I?"

They all nodded. "A bit," Nancy added.

"Fine, okay. I don't care. Who wants to take my place? Would you guys get those things off your heads!"

Walt and Angie did as requested. Nancy volunteered her services. "I'd like to give it a try."

"Do you know how?" It was a mean question, but so what if she was a bit hoarse?

Nancy was cool. "I believe I speak perfectly clear English."

"That's not what I meant. Do you know how close to stand to the mike and all that?"

"All what?" Nancy asked. "Yes, I know where to stand. Look, if you have to be up front —"

"I don't *have* to be anywhere. I asked a simple question and you get bent out of shape."

"I withdraw my suggestion," Nancy said tightly. "Keep the microphone."

We're doing it again, Mary Ellen thought. Her vocal cords *were* exhausted and Nancy's request was *not* unreasonable. For the good of the squad, she should give in. "I'm sorry, Nancy, I'm being greedy. Lead the cheers — you'll get a kick out of it."

"Mary Ellen!" a new voice called.

"Yes," she mumbled, glancing over her shoulder, finding only a blur of people.

"Thanks," Nancy smiled, instantly appeased, and walked away with Walt and Angie.

Cathleen Eismar was the one calling Mary Ellen's name. She huddled on the bottom row where Gemma had knelt. "What's it like being out in front of all these people?" Cathleen asked.

Was there a hint of bitterness in her voice? Mary Ellen decided she must be mistaken; Cathleen was not the jealous type. "It's better than being out on the field. What's up?"

"Nothing, just hanging out. Are you going to the party tonight?"

If one more person asks me that. . . . "No."

"That's a shame. Clara has a present she wanted me to give to Gemma."

"Really?" Mary Ellen smiled, pleased. Gemma was crazy about presents. "Gem's here tonight. She's sitting at the top. I bet you could find her if you looked."

"Actually, I don't have it with me."

"Is it in your car? I could run out with you before —"

"I'll have it at the party," Cathleen interrupted. "Can't you swing by for a few minutes?"

"I don't know," she muttered. Patrick wanted to go with her to the party but he was home with the flu. Of course, Walt would take her, if she asked, and he would also take her home. Then there was Pres. . . . Did she have the nerve to ask him? If he said no, it would be a slap in the face. She wasn't crazy about rejection. Still, transportation was not the major obstacle. The real question was whether she wanted to enter Vanessa's house. If it wasn't something for Gemma, it would have been easy to tell Cathleen to forget it. "Can I get it another time?"

"Clara wants Gemma to have it *right away*."

"What is it, anyway? Is it going to go bad?"

"Gee, Mary Ellen, I think it's a sweet gesture on my sister's part. But if you can't be bothered spending a few minutes of your precious time to pick up the gift, then maybe I should tell Clara to forget the whole thing."

Cathleen was acting awfully weird. "I'm sorry, I was just trying to figure out the best way to get it. Look, I'll see you at the party. I think that's great of Clara to give Gemma a present. Thank her for me."

They said polite good-byes and Mary Ellen

went searching for Walt, finding him sitting by himself at the far end of the team's empty bench. Catching his profile without his knowledge, she was struck by how lonely he looked. But then he became aware of her watching him and he smiled his energetic smile, the sad expression vanishing.

She hesitated, again searching for Pres. It would be silly to count on him when Walt would be a sure bet. "Walt, I have to pick up a present at Vanessa's party. Could you give me a ride?"

"Sure," he said enthusiastically.

She asked shyly, "Could you give me a ride home, too?" She *knew* he would.

"Sure," Walt said again, hardly believing his luck.

"You're a prince. But I hope I'm not putting you out. I don't plan on staying long."

"If I haven't had my fill, I can always go back," Walt said, knowing he'd rather be with Mary Ellen than a roomful of other people.

"I didn't know how you take your hot dogs," Pres said, walking toward her with a hot dog and a small Coke. "So I put everything on it."

"Thanks. That's perfect." In reality she hated mustard and relish. In fact, she disliked hot dogs altogether. She set the food on the bench beside Walt. "Let me give you the money —"

Pres stopped her. "No way. I'm suposed to be the rich kid in town. You want to give me a reputation as a penny pincher?"

She appreciated his generosity, particularly as she suddenly remembered that she didn't have a penny with her.

"Mary Ellen's going to the party, after all," Walt said.

Pres raised an eyebrow. Mary Ellen was sure — pretty sure — that he was glad. "We'll have to get together," he said casually. "I've decided to go, myself." By the look in his eyes, she knew what he meant by "getting together," and she found herself looking forward to it.

"Great," she said, aiming for the level of enthusiasm that would let him know she was interested, but not overly anxious. Why had she asked Walt? A minute more and Pres probably would have invited her.

"I'm going to give her a ride," Walt said.

Pres nodded, casting peculiar glances at him before turning back to her. Mary Ellen thought she was missing something. Hopefully, it was jealousy. "When did you change your mind?" he asked.

"Hardly a minute ago. Cathleen Eismar's sister has a present for Gemma that she wants me to pick up."

Pres appeared off-balance. "You only decided this moment?"

"Yes."

"That's odd. I talked to Vanessa ten minutes ago in the snack bar line. She told me you were going to the party."

Mary Ellen shrugged. "Vanessa's so conceited, she probably assumed that no one would miss one of her parties."

Pres was not convinced. "That's not how she sounded. She *knew* you were coming — she was *positive*. Cathleen must have told her."

CHAPTER

Mary Ellen heard the music before she saw the house — the familiar strains of Michael Jackson's voice and rhythms that were impossible to miss.

"Almost there," Walt said, not bothering with the jeep's brake as they swung into a turn draped in wraithlike branches. Mary Ellen threw a hand up to protect her face, grabbing the seat with her other hand to keep from bouncing out. They were late. The jeep had been slow starting, a major embarrassment to Walt despite her reassurances that there was no hurry. He seemed unusually keyed up tonight, anxious to please. "Have you ever been here before?" he asked.

"No, but now that I know exactly where she lives, I'll be extra careful to avoid the area."

They took another maniacal turn and she had to blink with the sudden glare. The modern tri-level house was a pool of light towering above rows of garden lamps that rimmed the property. The huge grassy backyard appeared to go all the way to the lake, a quarter mile away.

Walt parked and escorted her to the front door. A couple was making out in the shadows of the porch. Inside it was hot and loud. Pat Benatar had replaced Michael Jackson and was screaming that you shouldn't mess around with her. The living room was a mass of moving bodies. Yet despite the tight fit, the crowd had cleared a space for one couple. Mary Ellen saw to her amazement that one-half the couple was Nancy. She was dancing all right, nothing great, but the guy she was with was tearing up the floor. He wasn't doing bizarre spiral contortions — it was his *style*. It practically oozed out his snapping fingers, he had so much of it. He must be the guy Nancy had been talking about in practice.

The song came to an end. Without all the flailing limbs, they were able to make some headway into the house. Mary Ellen made a quick scan for Pres or Cathleen and didn't find either, accidentally locking eyes with Vanessa instead. Just her luck. Vanessa hurried toward her.

"Why, Mary Ellen!" she exclaimed, "I was wondering if you were going to stop by."

"Were you really?" she said, remembering Pres's remark at halftime.

"Yes." Vanessa didn't bat an eye. "Hello, Walt."

"Nice party you're having," he remarked.

"Isn't it wonderful?" Vanessa said, turning back to her. "I hope for tonight, at least, we can forget old feuds and enjoy each other's company."

"I didn't come here to fight," Mary Ellen said.

"Good!" Vanessa cheered. Oh brother, Mary Ellen thought.

"Except for the top floor, the entire house is open for play. There's plenty of food and all the punch you can drink," Vanessa told them.

"How is your club doing?" Walt asked.

"Fantastic! Two hundred people came to the first meeting."

"Two hundred new fans," Mary Ellen said deliberately. "Soon you'll be the big girl on campus."

"It's for a good cause," Vanessa said, catching her eyes, engaging her in a subtle power play and trying to stare her down. Mary Ellen remained undaunted.

"I'm sure it is," she replied sweetly, adding, "and I hear the voting for the homecoming court will be this week."

Vanessa nodded, not blinking. The pretense between them was rapidly disintegrating. "But that doesn't affect us. We'll both be on the court."

"But we can't both be *queen*, can we? That election's in less than three weeks. How much money will you have raised for the starving children by then?"

The corners of Vanessa's lips curled upwards, not so much in a smile as a sneer. "Lots."

"You'll probably get your picture in the paper, too."

"Probably. Does that bother you?" Vanessa asked sweetly.

"Not at all. As long as my picture is in the

paper again when *I'm* wearing the crown." Mary Ellen smiled and never took her eyes off Vanessa's.

"We should get two pistols," Walt joked, "and let you two settle it with a duel out front."

Vanessa broke eye contact and laughed. "Mary Ellen and I are merely teasing one another. Why, I'm sure we'll end up voting for each other. Isn't that right, Mary Ellen?"

"No," Mary Ellen said firmly.

Vanessa patted her on the back. "You're too much, Mary Ellen!" She turned her head toward the front door. "Would you please excuse me?"

"You're excused," Mary Ellen muttered, cringing at her touch.

When Vanessa was safely out of the way, Walt remarked, "I wonder what would happen if the two of you were locked together in a room overnight?"

"The survivor would be guilty of murder," Mary Ellen said, straightening her loose white blouse. The music came back on — The Pretenders.

"Can I get you a drink!?" Walt shouted as they retreated to a corner to avoid the dancers.

"Thanks, yes!!"

While she waited for Walt, she felt a tap on her shoulder.

"You made it after all!" Pres said. He had changed out of his cheerleading clothes into cutoffs, sandals, and a half-buttoned blue shirt. The muscles in his legs were as well developed and tan as those in his upper body. For an instant,

Patrick's face flashed in her mind before it was replaced with Pres's grin. Her stab of guilt was equally as brief.

"You look great!" he said, his eyes sweeping over her.

She touched her cheek lightly. "I have the same face I had at the game! You don't look bad yourself!"

Pres pulled her to the other side of the stairway, where they could hear each other talk. "What are you up to? Do you want to have some fun?"

She assumed he meant dancing. "Sure."

"Vanessa has a game room with one of my favorite arcade games — Star Destroyers. It's the real things, not a computer cartridge hooked up to a TV. Feel like playing?"

Mary Ellen disliked arcade games but she said, "Sounds neat."

Pres led her to the room. She hadn't forgotten Walt's drink or Cathleen's present — they merely weren't priorities at the moment. It was not often that Pres sought her out, and she was going to make the most of it. He wasn't Patrick. He didn't make her want to touch him and be touched, or to kiss his mouth softly and slowly, but Pres fit into her plans and Patrick didn't. She didn't like herself for feeling that way, but she was honest enough to admit what she *did* feel.

Vanessa watched Pres and Mary Ellen settle in front of the arcade screen with a mixture of joy and hatred. Mary Ellen was exactly where she wanted her to be, sitting down with distracting company about to engage in a distracting video screen exercise. She wouldn't even know what hit her.

Vanessa studied the specially prepared tray Cathleen carried in: the salt-saturated little sandwiches she had made that afternoon, the basketful of salty popcorn, the pretzels, and the alcohol-laced punch. One thing about salty food — you couldn't stop eating it once you started, even if you weren't hungry. Of course, it was always possible Mary Ellen or Pres would taste the alcohol in the drinks. But she was using vodka, camouflaged with fruit juices, and that was notoriously difficult to spot even for a seasoned drinker. Hopefully they would be so wrapped up in the game and each other, and so thirsty from the salt, that they wouldn't know and wouldn't care *what* was in the punch.

"Be sure to put the tray on the table to Mary Ellen's right, away from Pres," she told Cathleen, eyeing the couple at the far end of the room blowing up each other's planets. "She's our main target."

"Why don't *you* deliver the drinks?" Cathleen asked, not so dumb not to realize that there must be something in the punch.

"Impossible. She has to receive the drinks from someone she has no reason to distrust."

"But she'll ask about Clara's present."

"Do you have it out in the car?"

"Yes."

"Tell her that it's still at your house, that you were just about to go get it when I roped you into helping out. Act angry with me. You'll have no trouble stalling her — she's having fun."

Cathleen smiled. She was nervous but she was also enjoying herself. Vanessa knew she could trust her completely. After all, by having her give Mary Ellen the spiked punch, wasn't she making her directly responsible for the consequences? "When Mary Ellen starts to stagger about, are you going to ridicule her in front of everone?"

Vanessa shook her head. "I'm the only one who's going to know about it. A couple of hours from now, she'll owe me her undying gratitude."

Olivia wanted to go home. Nancy was dancing with Alex, Mary Ellen was conquering the universe with Pres, Angie was probably off making out with Marc, and here she sat waiting for someone who wasn't coming. She should have listened to her mom and settled for watching TV and going to bed early. There was no romance in her life. Who was she trying to fool? She had always been, and always would be, alone.

"Would you like some punch?" Walt asked, plopping down beside Olivia on the couch in the game room.

"Thanks." She swallowed the drink without tasting it.

"Did Michael Barnes show up?"

She hadn't spoken to him about her interest in Michael. He probably knew from having watched her with Michael at the cross-country meet. "No."

"That's a shame," he said sympathetically, and she couldn't help noticing how his eyes strayed to where Pres and Mary Ellen were laughing and drinking. She wasn't the only one feeling alone tonight.

"Walt, what time is it?"

"Ten-fifteen."

"Really?" Her mother had left her at the house with strict orders to call if she was going to be out past ten. "I've got to find a phone," she said, standing up.

"If you need a ride, let me know," Walt said.

She found a phone in the kitchen, but halfway through dialing the number she realized there was no reason for her to stay any longer. She would take Walt up on his offer and go home now. Feeling a dull ache in her chest, she replaced the receiver. This was the last party she was coming to this year.

"I hate you, Michael," she whispered.

The words were no sooner out of her mouth when he came through the back door, walked right by her, and began to make a sandwich with the tons of food spread across the kitchen table. Olivia took a deep breath and stayed in her corner. He put turkey, roast beef, tomatoes, lettuce, and pickles on his bread. He turned around and saw her.

"Calling somebody?" he asked between bites, indicating the phone beside her. She shook her head. He wore cords that had yet to lose their brand-new crease, and a thin, tan V-neck sweater with no shirt underneath. "I had the hardest time finding this place," he remarked, sprinkling salt on his sandwich.

"Couldn't you get directions from someone at the game?"

"I didn't go to the game."

"Oh, that's right, you hate football. It's just as well — we lost."

"A pity." He glanced around at the crowd of people, taking in the loud music and chatter. "Do you want to go for a walk?"

"But you just got here."

"I hate to overstay my welcome." He picked up a glass of punch, adding casually, "The moon is out."

"I love the moon," Olivia said.

Michael took her hand and they walked outside. Olivia felt her heart pounding in a normal, healthy way. It was the first time in all her sixteen years that she had been alone with a boy who held her hand and made her feel like a desirable young girl.

Mary Ellen was glad Star Destroyers didn't eat quarters. With the number of games they were playing, even Pres's generous allowance would have been hurting. She was surprised how much she was enjoying lasering his battle cruisers. She had won the last two games. Apparently she had an aptitude for video games. Either that or Pres was letting her win — she wasn't sure if he was, and she didn't care. She was having fun, though she was going to pay for this night on the scale. She couldn't stop eating the food near her. And she hoped the punch wasn't loaded with calories. It must be the heat — her thirst was insatiable.

"What did you say?" she giggled.

"You dropped your joystick."

"My *what*?"

"Your firing stick," Pres said. "You've been shooting for the last minute without it."

"I have?" Mary Ellen frowned at the screen. He might have a point. He had ten ships left to her one. She wasn't going to win this game. Searching for her joystick, her right hand strayed to the punch. "Want a drink, Pres?" He shook his head. "Have a pretzel, then?"

"This week is my health week."

"Your *what*?"

He smiled at her amazement. "One week a month I eat only fruits and vegetables. But next week I'll be back on junk food."

"It almost *is* next week," she mumbled, looking at her watch, unable to wipe the fog off the crystal. "It's almost twelve o'clock. Have one drink, at least. Have three."

He smiled again. She must be pretty witty tonight. Cathleen came by again with a tray.

"How are we doing here?" she asked, setting down six sparkling punches and a plate of sandwiches on a nearby coffee table.

"Great!" Mary Ellen exclaimed. "Couldn't be better. Hey, Cathleen, why are you helping Vanessa?"

"I told you, she roped me into it," Cathleen replied, sounding annoyed. Mary Ellen couldn't blame her. Vanessa was always making people do things they didn't want to do. She was a bad person, simply awful.

"Where's Gemma's present?"

"It's at home. I'll get it for you as soon as I finish serving these drinks."

Mary Ellen vaguely remembered her having said that before. "Take your time. Pres and I aren't in a hurry."

Pres stared at her briefly — rather strangely, she thought. Then he said to Cathleen, "Give me a glass of that punch, will you?"

"Have some of mine," Mary Ellen said, reaching for her glass. But Cathleen beat her to it, removing a cup from her tray and handing it to Pres. Then he did the most peculiar thing. He smelled it. How gross! Did he drink with his nose during his health food week? She tried not to laugh, but it didn't do a bit of good.

"Is something wrong?" Cathleen asked.

Pres took a sip, thought for a moment, then shook his head. "No, nothing. Thanks for the drink." When Cathleen was gone, he asked, "Do you want to dance? You must be tired of this game."

She would have loved to dance, yet it suddenly seemed such an effort to get up. It was nice being alone with him in the corner. She shook her head, moving closer to him.

"I like you, Pres," she whispered, lightly scratching his arm with her fingernails.

"Really?" he asked uneasily.

"I'm not saying that just to please you." She turned her head to a convenient angle, in case he wanted to kiss her. "I mean, I really like you." She squeezed his arm. "You have a nice body, too."

Pres knew something was strange about Mary Ellen. He had carefully smelled and tasted that she had been drinking and it was straight punch — no liquor. Yet she was *acting* drunk. But Pres never turned away from what he wanted and right now he wanted Mary Ellen. He took her in his arms and kissed her, first gently and then with more feeling. Her arms went up around his neck and she sighed, but it was obvious to Pres the sigh came more from sleepiness than passion.

Pres pushed Mary Ellen away. There were some times, some circumstances, where taking advantage of another person was really crummy.

"Mary Ellen?"

She stared into his dreamy, dark eyes. "Yes?"

"Let's play some more."

"I'll play any game you want."

He pointed at the video screen. "Let's play Star Destroyers."

Mary Ellen eased back into her chair, picking up her joystick. He was not rejecting her — he was merely shy. She could *feel* his passion. Later, they would be in each other's arms.

Mary Ellen had another sandwich and punch and blew away half a solar system. It was a *great* party.

CHAPTER

"Where did you learn to dance like that?" Nancy asked Alex as they sat down, out of breath after another marathon session with the ear-splitting music. Thankfully, in the game room it was quieter.

Alex ran his fingers through his hair. "Clubs in London. When I wasn't playing, me and my mates would make the rounds Friday and Saturday night. Some nights, we never got to bed. Those were good times."

She could hear his nostalgia. "You miss it, don't you?"

"Not tonight," he grinned, grabbing a discarded drink off the floor and downing it in a gulp, "not dancing with you. Don't sell yourself short. You move beautifully."

"I would hope so. We work at it all week in practice."

"Yeah." Something in his tone made her sit up.

"What is it?"

"I didn't say anything."

"It's what you *didn't* say."

"I don't know what you're talking about." He was searching for another drink. She grabbed his arm and made him look at her.

"You don't like our routines, do you?"

He opened his mouth to speak, hesitated, then nodded. "They're not as good as they could be."

She'd had the same thought. Nevertheless, she felt defensive. "No one's been ordering you to go to the pep rallies."

Her anger evaporated as swiftly as it had bubbled up. "I'm sorry," she said, "I always feel I should defend the squad."

It was funny, they all still fought with each other. There were still times when she couldn't stand Mary Ellen or Olivia or Pres, but she didn't want anyone else badmouthing them.

"I hate to think we're lousy. Why, we have the prelims for the state cheerleaders competition next Saturday afternoon," she said.

"*You* are not lousy. I said your *routines* are not as good as they could be. You can't take your performance too personally. If you do, you'll fall so in love with it that you'll be unable to change it." He eased back into the couch. "Last week in biology you mentioned that you didn't do well in camp. Do you know why?"

"We *did* well. Our competition just did better."

"How so?"

"They were more exciting, more . . . contemporary. I was so nervous I could scarcely concentrate on our own routine, never mind somebody else's. But I do remember thinking that a lot of the kids must have spent the summer watching rock and new wave videos on MTV."

Alex nodded. "I don't want to criticize your Mrs. Engborg. With her track record, she must be an excellent coach, but she may be old-fashioned. Trends change quickly, in music and clothes as well as dance —" He was interrupted by a loud giggle at the end of the room. Mary Ellen was laughing uncontrollably. Alex pointed in their direction. "Is she your captain?"

"Mary Ellen? Yes."

"If Mary Ellen and everyone else on the squad agreed upon a change, would Mrs. Engborg go along with it?"

"Yes, as long as it wasn't too bizarre. She encourages our creativity. But to get us all to agree upon a change would take a small miracle." She nodded toward Mary Ellen. "Our leader is a hard sell. And like I said, we don't have many days before competition starts. I doubt we could learn a whole new routine."

"I'm not suggesting you start from scratch. A few changes could make a world of difference. The frills sell the product. I'll give it some thought."

"Okay," she said, not sure she wanted him to bother. Alex was a wonderful guy but she couldn't help feeling he was butting in where he shouldn't. Unless they did poorly in the prelim, the others wouldn't be open to an outsider's help. And if they *did* poorly, they wouldn't need help because they would be out of the running.

Alex looked at Nancy warmly and asked, "Can I drive you home?"

Nancy moved away slightly. "Walt is going to drop me off, but thanks." She liked Alex, was attracted to him physically more than she had been to any boy since Rick. But he also put her off. The earring, the loud clothes, and the bleached hair made her uneasy. He might be more than she could cope with.

When Alex reached for her, she didn't back away but she felt herself tightening. She was afraid . . . of what she didn't know. But his mouth on hers was gentle, undemanding, as if he sensed her fear and was trying to allay it. Nancy relaxed and returned his kiss as gently as it was given, but she found herself wanting more.

Alex pulled her up from the sofa on which they had been sitting and they went outside for one last dance. Nancy was glad Walt was driving her home, because no way was she ready, if she ever would be, to introduce Alex to her father. But her thoughts went to the next Saturday night, when they would be together again.

"Pres is becoming suspicious," Cathleen said to Vanessa as they huddled by the back door of the kitchen. It was getting late — after midnight — and the crowd was thinning. Vanessa's awe of Mary Ellen's ability to hold her liquor continued to grow.

"It's been both a blessing and a curse that he hasn't been drinking," Vanessa said. "He hasn't had a chance to taste the alcohol, but he's more alert to the changes in Mary Ellen. The glass you let him sample was plain, right?"

"Yes."

"That was quick thinking." Some of her own genius must be rubbing off, Vanessa thought. "We can't wait any longer. We've got to get Pres out of the picture. Go back upstairs and tell him some of the guys on the team want to talk to him. Be vague — don't tell him which guys. Lead him down here to me and I'll take care of him. Then go and sit with Mary Ellen. Talk to her about *anything*. Stay with her and keep her there.

"When she finally asks you where the bathroom is, and she will, take her to the bathroom in the master bedroom on the third floor. That room's door will be shut but unlocked. You can open it for Mary Ellen and point out the bathroom on the other side of the bed, but *don't follow her into the room*. This is very important. Leave her and hurry back downstairs."

"Then what?" Cathleen asked.

"There isn't time now for explanations. Get Pres. Hurry!"

Watching Cathleen run off, Vanessa thought of what would happen when Mary Ellen hurried through the master bathroom door. The prospect was so deliciously wicked, she burst into laughter.

The yellow moon shone on the mirror of the lake. Except for occasional pockets of cool air that seemed to pass through their very skin as they strolled the water's edge, the night was warm and humid, saturated with the smell of daisies and grass. Olivia realized her shoes were soaked with mud, but didn't mind. Michael was telling her about when he had scuba dived to the bottom of the lake last summer.

Michael stared out over the rippling water. It was peaceful and quiet, Vanessa's party music a half mile about an hour ago. He added, "It left the house about an hour ago. He added, "It was an interesting way to get away from it all without having to travel a huge distance."

"Do you like to be alone?"

He plopped onto the ground, plucking a blade of grass and chewing the tip. Knowing she was dirtying her skirt, she didn't hesitate to sit beside him.

"Most of the time," he said.

They talked quietly.

She told him about her heart operation, and quite a few other things about her life. He was an excellent listener. However, except for describing his scuba diving adventure, he hadn't volunteered anything personal. He hadn't mentioned the loss of his parents.

"I suppose you were alone a lot as a child," he said.

"I got used to it," she said. "I don't know if I ever liked it."

"It has its advantages."

Far along the shore, Olivia heard giggles, male and female — a couple having fun together. Michael was such a serious person, it was difficult to imagine him having fun. Not that *she* was anybody's comic relief.

"Then why do you work so hard running? By being the best, you're only attracting attention to yourself."

"I don't run to impress others, but to prove to myself that I can accomplish what I set my mind to do."

"Do you always succeed?"

He flashed a brief grin, picking up a rock and tossing it into the lake. "Not always. I'm not a machine, you know."

She smiled. "How would I know? You run like one."

He seemed to like the comparison. "I probably act like one, too, sometimes."

"Not at all. You're just very reserved."

He nodded, staring at her now, the moonlight bright in his eyes. "And you're the same way, Olivia. That's why I like talking to you."

"You do?" She wished she didn't sound as amazed as she felt. "I like you . . . talking to you, too."

He turned away and seemed to think about that for a minute. Finally, he asked, "How would you like to —"

"Is that Olivia!?" Angie's voice — it had never sounded so irritating — exclaimed. She and Michael jumped quickly to their feet. Approaching from the opposite direction of the party, hand-in-hand, were Marc Filanno and Angie.

"Friends of yours?" Michael whispered.

"Great friends," she muttered, disgusted. Michael had been on the verge of asking her out. Angie let go of Marc and threw both her hands into the air.

"It *is* Olivia! I never imagined the day would come when I would catch you lying on the shore of the lake late at night with a boy!" Angie was gently teasing, but it angered Olivia.

"Stop that, Angie, you're embarrassing them," Marc said — the understatement of the *year*. He was a familiar face, often detouring from his vending machine route to pick up Angie after practice. Short and thin with curly dark hair and a thick moustache above a ready smile, he was not so much handsome as he was appealing. Moonlit droplets sparkled around his head. Olivia realized that both Marc and Angie's hair was soaked.

"Hello," Michael said quietly, apparently not troubled by the interruption.

"Michael, this is Marc," Olivia cut in. "Marc, meet Michael." As they shook hands, she added, "How was the water, Angie?"

Angie glanced at Marc who looked at the ground. "Fine," she said quietly, brushing back her wet hair, trying to hide it.

"You went swimming?" Michael asked innocently.

Neither answered immediately. Olivia asked, "Can't you get in trouble for skinny dipping?"

"Who said we went skinny dipping?" Angie asked quickly.

"Hey, why *don't* we?" Marc asked.

Olivia could not even conceive of such an act. Fortunately neither Michael nor Angie looked excited about the suggestion. The discussion was interrupted anyway, for Pres joined them.

"Have any of you seen the guys on the team?"

Pres asked, coming out of the warm darkness from the direction of Vanessa's house, sandals in hand.

"No," Angie said. "Which guys are you looking for?"

Pres appeared rather lost, unusual for him. "I don't know. Vanessa said some of the guys wanted to speak to me and that they were down by the water. But you're the first people I've seen."

"No one's passed this way," Olivia said.

"Oh, Olivia," Pres said, "Your mother called when I was talking to Vanessa in the kitchen. She's been waiting up for you. Better hurry back. Vanessa thought she sounded upset."

Her mother! She had totally forgotten! Vanessa had undoubtedly understated the truth to her — "sounded upset." Her mother had probably notified the National Guard. She turned to Michael. "She worries about me constantly. It's her main occupation. Can we talk . . . another time?"

"Sure. I'll walk you back."

"That's odd none of you have seen any of the team," Pres said. "Maybe I should head back, too — check on how Mary Ellen's doing."

The ceiling kept sagging to the floor. It would have been a novel optical phenomenon if Mary Ellen's stomach hadn't been doing the same. Her sickness had hit suddenly and was getting worse. She wished Cathleen would shut up. Every word she spoke grated on her nerves. Something was not right somewhere. . . .

". . . He hasn't called in five days," Cathleen

was saying. "The last time we went out, he was so rude."

"Cathleen," Mary Ellen interrupted, "where's Pres?"

"He's talking to some guys on the team. Don't you remember?"

She didn't remember and couldn't understand why she didn't. Her thoughts refused to form a straight line, wheeling like colliding frisbees under a strobe light. "Get him for me, would you please?" she whispered.

"What's the matter, are you sick? You don't look so hot."

She tried to stand but her knees had silly putty for joints. She fell back into her chair. "I must be getting the flu. Where's the bathroom?" she asked weakly.

Cathleen took her arm and helped her up. "Why, you poor dear, I'll show you where one is."

Mary Ellen tried to walk without assistance but the furniture kept getting in her way. Short-circuited as her brain was, she was nonetheless aware of the eyes that followed as Cathleen led her upstairs.

The overhead light on the third floor hallway stung Mary Ellen's eyes. Cathleen turned the knob on the bedroom door, and pointed to a closed door on the far side of the darkened room. "There's the bathroom. There shouldn't be anyone in it. I'll leave you now. Hope you feel better."

Mary Ellen nodded absently, all her attention focused on reaching the bathroom door. She staggered around the huge bed, reached out a shaky hand, grasped the handle, and turned it. The light switch clicked under her groping fingers, the sudden glare making her wince as it reflected off a large mirror. Throwing a hand over her eyes, she pushed inside, slamming the door shut at her back. Vaguely, as though it were coming from far away, she heard a peculiar cracking noise. But it was not important. All that mattered was how sick she felt.

Standing outside the closed master bedroom door, Vanessa sucked in her breath. The crucial moment had come. Everything had gone as planned. There remained only one detail still to be fulfilled — documented evidence of tonight's irresponsible behavior had to be collected and stored away until the time when it could do the most good.

Mary Ellen felt much better. Splashing cold water on her face, she squinted at one corner of the mirror. A pile of shattered colored plaster lay on the floor by the door. Had she bumped into something on the way in? Turning from the reflection, she knelt by the sharp-edged chips. It looked like a vase, or what had been a vase.

There came a knock at the door. Mary Ellen looked up, her head cleared but still aching. "Yes?"

"Who's in there?"

Vanessa! Curse the moment she had decided to go to this party! She looked for another door, not finding one. The window? She was on the third floor, she would break her neck. Vanessa continued to knock.

"Whoever you are, you better get out immediately. This is my parent's bathroom."

Mary Ellen remained silent, praying Vanessa would go away. No such luck.

"Did you hear me in there?" Vanessa demanded.

"I heard you," Mary Ellen mumbled in resignation, opening the door. Vanessa took one quick look at her, saw the broken plaster on the floor, and turned a glowering red.

"That's my mother's Swiss vase! Did you break it?"

Mary Ellen remembered the cracking sound she had heard when going through the door. She considered lying before realizing it would be useless. "I accidentally banged into it. I'm sorry."

Vanessa crouched by the broken vase, holding it as though it were an injured child. "My mother's going to kill me," she whispered.

"I'll take full responsibility."

Vanessa stabbed her with her eyes. "For your information, Mary Ellen, my parents don't know I'm having this party. How can you take responsibility? You're not even supposed to *be* here."

"I said, I'm sorry. How . . . how much did it cost?"

"Five hundred dollars! Do you have that much? I do, but it's all that I have." Vanessa slammed one of the large pieces against the opposite wall, giving full vent to her anger. "How could you have been so clumsy? That vase has sat there perfectly safe for three years!"

"Cathleen brought me up here and —"

"Oh, blame it on Cathleen!"

"I'm not *blaming* it on Cathleen," she said,

fighting to keep her voice even. If she started to cry, Vanessa would run for her Polaroid. Later, though, she knew she would cry. "I'll give your parents the money. I'll call them tomorrow . . . explain what happened."

"Didn't you hear me? If you call my parents, they'll find out about the party." She ground a piece on the floor into white dust. "*I'll* have to take the blame. *I'll* have to pay for it."

"I'll pay you back."

"When?"

"Soon. I'll pay you in installments." Mary Ellen felt tears coming to her eyes. I'm not going to cry, she thought. Not in front of Vanessa. Not if I die holding the tears back.

Vanessa closed her eyes, and took a deep breath. When she spoke next, her voice was low, and Mary Ellen did see the glint in her eyes. "I suppose that's how it will have to be. I'll give my mother the money, tell her I accidentally bumped into the vase, and you can pay me back. But I wanted a signed I.O.U."

Mary Ellen nodded. It was hard to talk. She felt too sick, too confused.

"Your payments will start next Friday — twenty-five dollars a week. At that rate, it will take me half a year to get my money back. And I'm going to charge interest. I think that's only fair."

"But . . ." Mary Ellen began, choking on the implications. Her parents couldn't help her. They could barely make ends meet. She would have to get a job, but she couldn't work *and* be on the squad. She would have to quit the squad! This was a nightmare. Why couldn't she wake up?

"But, what?"

"Nothing. Write your I.O.U., and I'll sign it."

"Don't grumble at me. *I'm* not the one who broke the vase. I'm not exactly thrilled about what happened."

"Okay, I'm sorry." There, she had said it again. She hated Vanessa . . . and herself, and the world.

Vanessa went for a pen and paper. Mary Ellen took one last look at the broken vase and stepped out of the bathroom and sat on the bed. Vanessa returned a moment later and sat beside her, composing out loud.

"I, Mary Ellen Kirkwood, agree to pay Vanessa Barlow twenty weekly installments of twenty-five dollars each in compensation for a vase I broke in Vanessa Barlow's house on the night of October 1. I understand that this note is legally binding and that each payment is due each Friday until all twenty payments have been made, starting October 9." Vanessa thrust the paper in her face. "Read it and sign."

Mary Ellen examined it as closely as her aching head would permit. One would have thought Vanessa was a lawyer, it read so well. "I'll sign it on the condition that this is kept private."

"Agreed," Vanessa said.

"I want that in writing," Mary Ellen demanded.

Vanessa glared at her. "I don't care what you want. You'll sign that as it's written."

There was no alternative. Picking up the pen and signing the I.O.U., Mary Ellen felt like she was signing her life away. But she was tired and confused, and the success she had always dreamed of seemed impossible to ever achieve.

After dropping Nancy off, Walt drove Mary Ellen home and tried to break through her silence and depression. He couldn't figure out what was bothering her, and after a few attempts at conversation, he too was silent. When they reached her house, he opened the door for her, knowing not to try to touch her.

"Thanks for the ride, Walt," she mumbled and ran toward the door.

Walt watched her for a minute and then drove off, wishing he could have thought of something to say to her.

When Mary Ellen got to her door, a figure moved out of the shadows. Mary Ellen caught her breath in fear, until she realized it was Patrick.

"I thought you were sick, Patrick," she said. "You scared the life out of me."

"I felt better and I wanted to make sure you got home all right. I just wanted to see you for a few minutes, Mary Ellen. I hate it when you're out with other guys. I want to be the one you're with."

Mary Ellen felt herself weakening at his nearness, as she always did. The humiliation and confusion and sickness of the night washed over her, and she let herself be drawn into Patrick's arms. She rested against his chest and wept softly, feeling a wonderful safeness leaning against him. When he kissed her, she let herself forget about everything but the feelings he evoked in her —

the wanting and needing — and she moved closer to him.

When he felt her tears on his face, he drew back. "Mary Ellen! What is it?" He brushed the teardrops off her cheeks and kissed her eyes gently.

"Patrick, I can't talk now. Just hold me."

After Mary Ellen had gone, Vanessa went to the hall closet and got a broom and dust pan to clean up the mess. She also collected a second vase she had bought that afternoon for fifteen dollars, identical in every respect to the one Mary Ellen had broken. Putting the new vase in its proper place, far from where the other one had been minutes ago, she sang, "Here comes the queen."

CHAPTER

It was their turn next. Nancy didn't know whether to rejoice or cry. It would be good to begin and get it over with, but not at this *exact* minute. Bad as the waiting was, making an error would be far worse.

"If these are the prelims," Nancy said to Olivia, "I can't wait to see how the finals feel."

"We might not have to worry about that," Olivia said gloomily.

They were sitting in the last row of the Chetfield College gymnasium, the site of the annual State Cheerleading Competition (SCC). Beneath them were hundreds of fellow competitors, the stands a rainbow of uniforms. Also present were family and friends. But none were there to cheer for them. Mrs. Engborg had called their parents and requested that they not come, thinking they would only add to the pressure on the squad. Nancy wouldn't have minded having her mother in the stands, but it was true that having her dad present would have made her nervous. Except for Walt and Pres, who had come separately in Pres's Porsche, Mrs. Engborg had driven them all the hundred miles south to the college early this morning. It was only two o'clock and the day already felt a century old.

"What do you think of this squad?" Nancy asked Olivia, referring to the Wickfield Warriors — league rivals — who were performing on the basketball floor to the tune of Bowie's "Let's Dance."

"They're good."

"You said that about the last squad," Nancy said with irritation.

"They're *all* good."

Nancy contemplated joining the rest of the squad, who were warming up in the lobby. There wasn't much time, and Olivia and she could both use another stretch, but she was trying to avoid Mary Ellen. Now was not the time for arguments and Mary Ellen had been in the foulest of moods all week. It made no sense. If I'd just been voted onto the homecoming court, Nancy thought, I'd be ecstatic.

Despite having expected nothing different, Nancy had been hurt at being passed over. Probably what had cut the deepest was that Angie had been picked as one of the five princesses. Angie was a nice girl, and Nancy wished her all the best, but there were literally dozens of girls in the school prettier than Angie. Nancy Goldstein was one of them. Angie herself had said as much — it was easy to be humble when you were a winner. The whole contest was a joke to Angie.

Nancy felt almost rigid with tension. Today was enough to tie anyone in knots. First this competition, and later, her date with Alex. Still, despite the pressures, she was exactly where she wanted to be. All her worrying made her feel more alive.

The Warriors and their music finished together. The routines were judged on a scale of one to ten by six cheerleading coaches from various parts of the state. Mrs. Engborg was not among their number. It it happened that the judge's own school was performing, he or she was replaced by an alternate. A perfect score was sixty, but the highest so far today had been fifty-one. Only three squads out of the twenty-six in the gym would get to the finals. The third place team had a score of forty-eight. The Warrior's marks flashed on the scoreboard — forty-three. They were out of it.

"What did they do wrong?" Olivia asked in amazement.

"They looked nervous." Nancy stood. "Come, let's join the rest of the squad. It's time."

Pres wanted to look strong to impress the girls. He figured he might as well fool *them*, since he had been unable to fool himself. Inside, he felt on the verge of an adrenaline overdose. The second he stopped stretching, his muscles would begin to tighten. The drive down with Walt had not been the most relaxing. Walt had wanted to discuss Pres and Mary Ellen's relationship. Initially Pres had feigned innocence, but Walt had laughed so hard that Pres had finally admitted to liking her a little bit. On the surface, Walt had taken the confession well. Pres had to wonder if Walt wasn't simply waiting until after the competition to kill him.

"Nancy and Olivia should be here," Mary Ellen complained to the boys, as she paced like a caged animal. Through the lobby windows, she could see that it was raining heavily. Summer had vanished on the dark front of a Canadian storm. Mary Ellen had already mentioned how much she hated rain. Something besides the competition was bothering her. If it wasn't for Walt, Pres would have offered her a ride home to get to the bottom of it. There was the chance she wasn't upset about anything. Maybe this was the way she really was. It made him wonder.

"They can both read a clock. They'll be here," Mrs. Engborg said, sitting on a folding chair, drinking coffee. "Stop that pacing, Mary Ellen."

Angie and Walt laughed loudly. Mrs. Engborg quieted them with a scowl as Olivia and Nancy came out of the gym.

"How did the Warriors do?" Pres asked.

Nancy gave a thumbs-down. "Forty-three."

"That's great," Pres said. "One less team to worry about."

"That's terrible," Mary Ellen said. "The judges are giving lousy scores. They're getting tired. It would have been better to have gone on earlier instead of last."

Mrs. Engborg disagreed. "Don't fool yourself — the time of day doesn't affect the judges. The Warriors did poorly because they hadn't practiced enough. All of you have practiced thoroughly, so you will do well."

The speakers erupted into life. "Tarenton High!"

"Who goes to school there?" Walt asked Angie.

Angie shook her head. "Never heard of the place."

Mrs. Engborg stood and shook each of their hands. "Do your best and you'll make me proud."

And while you're at it, Pres thought, be sure to qualify. As he trailed the others onto the basketball floor and sought his position at the center of their T formation, he could feel the eyes of the audience willing him to make a mistake. It was understandable. Tarenton High had been too successful in the past. No one rooted for the big shot. Yet those had been different squads with different people. He would have preferred being the underdog.

Their music began — Tony Basil's "Micky." The song had energy even if it was cutesy. As had been the case from the beginning, their routine was divided into four sections. However, unlike when they performed before their home crowd, they did not drag out the initial pompon riffling. The judges were not, in Mrs. Engborg's opinion, impressed with flash. Quickly they shifted into the girls' interweaving cartwheels. To an untrained observer, Pres knew, it looked as though Walt and he were doing little. This was not true. As the girls spun blindly, Walt and he controlled their timing. If a mistake occurred, it was seldom the girls' fault. As Mary Ellen, Angie, Nancy, and Olivia toppled through their 360-

degree arcs, Pres was conscious of how close their feet were to rearranging his nose. Everything was happening so fast, he was forgetting his nervousness. In fact, he began to feel the opposite — confident and exhilarated. They slipped into part three, where the girls vaulted off their backs. It was important to the judges that the two who were in the air land in synchrony. Equally important was that Walt and he put exactly the required spring into the girls' launch. The only thing worse than too little was too much.

They made it through the vaults without a hitch. Pres could taste a qualifying score. Now for the grand finale, their upright T. In many respects, this was the most demanding part. Once Walt and he established the foundation for the girls to stand on, they could not move a millimeter. He had lain awake more than one night, wondering what would happen to Mary Ellen, who crowned the T, if he had a sudden muscle twitch. It would be a long fall. Fortunately, their coordination held solid. He was both surprised and gratified to hear the roar of the crowd as the song finished. Mary Ellen jumped down and skipped to the mike to smile and thank the judges. Straightening from his crouched position, he discovered the three-minute exercise had stained his cheerleading shirt with sweat. Now came the best or worst part — the score.

"I think we made it," Nancy breathed, as they gathered at the side of the court and stared at the scoreboard.

"Let's hope so," Mary Ellen nodded, her face flushed.

"What do we need?" Walt asked casually.

"Better than forty-eight," Nancy said.

The number flashed in lights the instant the speaker called out, "Tarenton High, forty-nine. Third place."

Pres had braced himself for disappointment, so it took him a moment to drop his guard. He felt more relief than joy. They hadn't won anything, yet. There was still next Saturday, when the competition would be even tougher. On the other hand, he refused to worry about it now, and joined the back slapping and hugging. He even gave Mrs. Engborg a kiss on the cheek. He must have been feeling pretty happy.

On the way out to the parking lot, laughing and rehashing their greatness, the rain giving them a brief respite, Walt pulled Pres aside.

"How about if on the way back I swap places with Mary Ellen?" he asked. "I want to discuss next week's strategy with Mrs. Engborg."

Walt wasn't interested in strategy. There was no such thing in cheerleading competitions. He was just showing Pres that there were no hard feelings about Mary Ellen. "If that's what you want," Pres said, clasping his hand warmly. "You're a good guy, Walt."

"We'll have to sharpen our transitions," Pres was saying as they soared toward Tarenton, the windshield wipers struggling with the downpour while rolling green fields and browning leaf trees rushed by. Mary Ellen was scarcely aware of the weather or the scenery. Pres continued, "We need more speed. Maybe we should discard the pompon section altogether. What do you think?"

"I don't know," she said quietly.

"I'd like to change our song . . . find something less quaint."

"Sounds good," she whispered.

"If nothing else, we get a shot at the best squads in the state. I feel pretty good about that, don't you?"

"Great." She didn't want to, especially in front of Pres, but it just happened. She burst out crying.

"Oh," was all he said, pulling to the side of the road and turning off the engine. He gave her a minute and a box of Kleenex from the glove compartment. She needed both. Finally he asked, "Do you want to talk about it?"

She nodded. She needed to talk to someone. She hadn't been able to tell Patrick. Afraid that they might yell at her — or worse, feel obligated to pay the money — she hadn't told her parents either . . . or Gemma. It would break her little sister's heart. "I have to quit the squad," she sniffed.

"What?"

"I have to get a job to pay for a vase I broke at Vanessa's house. The payments are due every Friday, twenty-five dollars for twenty weeks. I didn't even see the blasted thing but I signed the I.O.U. because I didn't know what else to do."

"Whoa, slow down. Back up and start at the beginning."

She began at the party at the point when Cathleen had led Pres away, finishing with the wording and signing of the I.O.U. "So I'm stuck," she said in conclusion. "If I don't pay, Vanessa will probably take me to court." It had been a relief to say it, particularly to Pres, who had listened closely without interrupting. But now he had questions.

"You say you had an attack of the flu? How did you feel the next day?"

"Sick. I had the worst headache."

He surprised her. "Maybe what you had was a hangover."

"How? I didn't drink anything except punch."

"From *alcohol* in the punch. When was the last time you drank?"

"I don't remember."

"It wasn't in this lifetime, was it?"

She hadn't had much chance. "No."

"Don't be ashamed. I didn't ask it to embarrass you. The fact is you don't know what alcohol tastes like — and you wouldn't have known if the punch *was* spiked, though I smelled alcohol on your breath. With that couple smoking nearby I couldn't be sure, though. That's why I asked Cathleen for a glass of the punch."

"Was there alcohol in it?"

"Not that I could tell. But thinking back, I realize Cathleen took the glass I sampled off *her* tray, quickly, like she didn't want me to touch yours."

His insinuation was clear. "But why would Cathleen do that?"

Pres was thoughtful. "At the party, both Cathleen and Vanessa told me a few of the guys on the team wanted to talk to me out back. But there was no one there."

"Are you saying they conspired to get me drunk, get you out of the way, and have me bang into the vase?" Even as she outlined the bizarre scenerio, she knew it was *true*. Deep inside, a hatred that would not burn out until revenged began to spark.

"It's only a possibility," Pres interrupted her murderous thoughts, "one that would be difficult to prove. Though I must admit, you were acting awfully cheerful for someone on the verge of an illness."

His remark triggered a vague memory of kissing him. Was it real or part of a dream? "How cheerful was I?" she asked carefully.

He smiled. "You were a lot of fun. But let's discuss that in a minute. We have to figure out how to handle this. And as far as I can see, there's only one way. I'll have to take care of the payments."

Mary Ellen breathed a sigh of relief inside. She hated herself, but she realized that she had been hoping Pres would say that. How low can I get, she thought. But she forced herself to say, "Absolutely not. You'd have to work extra hours for your father, and I know you'd hate that." She scarcely breathed, fearing he'd agree with her. Somehow, she'd find a way to pay Pres back. It would be a lot easier than paying Vanessa.

Pres took her hand. "Look, it's the logical move. The squad can't break up. You'd only get minimum wage at a job in Tarenton. Dad and I don't see eye-to-eye, but he pays me fifteen bucks an hour. A couple of hours work more a week won't kill me."

"I don't want either of us to pay that beast a cent."

"You signed the I.O.U. If you go around telling people you got drunk as a result of an elaborate plot, they'll laugh in your face. Let's give Vanessa her money and hope she lives up to her end of the bargain and keeps it private."

He was right. He was her knight in shining armor. Framed by the blurred green landscape filtering through the window, she saw him as a blond-haired Lancelot. "Why are you doing this?"

"To keep the squad together."

"Oh."

He must have heard her disappointment. He touched her shoulder. The car seemed suddenly cramped, not uncomfortably so. "And because I like you, Mary Ellen. I want to help you."

She bent her head, took his hand, and held it in her lap. "I like you, Pres."

"Do you?" He sounded unsure of himself.

She smiled. "Can't you tell?" She drew a nail across the inside of his palm. His fingers twitched. "Does that tickle?"

"I don't know which question to answer."

She brushed the hair out of his eyes. "The first one."

He took back his hand and moved closer. For an instant, she almost giggled. It was just like in the movies. The windows really were getting steamy. "Yes," he said, "I could tell. You're not always subtle, Mary Ellen, but I don't mind that."

She could feel his breath. It smelled like peppermints. He put his arm around her and she leaned into him. "Sometimes, it doesn't pay to be subtle," she said.

He smiled. "There. We agree."

"When I wasn't in my right state of mind at the party," she said softly, "what did I say?"

He tugged lightly at her curls. "You said I had a nice body."

"No!"

"Yes." Pres grinned, watching Mary Ellen's discomfort out of the corner of his eye.

"Well, you do have a nice body," she said defensively. The rain was a waterfall on the roof of the Porsche, making it extra cozy to be inside. "What else happened?"

"I kissed you."

She sat up, touched his lower lip with her finger. "Don't you want to kiss me now?"

He pulled her toward him. A race car was not necessarily designed for making out, but neither of them could complain. As always, she thought of Patrick as Pres kissed her. But Pres was going to pay Vanessa. Patrick wasn't. And tearing Patrick from her mind, she concentrated on Pres.

CHAPTER

Vanessa Barlow was bored. It was raining and she couldn't lie out by the lake and deepen her tan for the upcoming homecoming court pictures. Equally tiresome, Cathleen was on the phone. Cathleen was like Steve Dextrile — their every remark was predictable.

"Did Mary Ellen make the first payment?" Cathleen asked.

"Yesterday, yeah," Vanessa said, studying her figure in the mirror. The glass must have developed ripples when it was hot, it made her look fat. "Don't worry, the twenty-five dollars probably wiped out half of her savings. She'll be job hunting soon."

"What will you do if she misses a payment?"

Vanessa sighed. She had told Cathleen about the I.O.U. in the hope it would shut her up. It had done the opposite. She had no desire to explain that Mary's Ellen's payments were of no significance. Come next Monday, copies of the I.O.U. along with appropriate supporting rumors, would be circulated at school. That would be four days before the homecoming queen election. No one would vote for a suspected drunk.

"Cathleen," she said, ignoring the question, "how much money have you collected for Food for the Forgotten?" Yesterday's club meeting had been rough. The students had become restless for definite plans to raise money to donate to UNICEF. She had made several reasonable suggestions: contact local businesses, talk to churches, ask their parents. But the ideas had not gone over well. To counteract the lack of enthusiasm, she had made the bold — foolish, she now realized — statement that she would match, dollar for dollar, through her own efforts, every contribution from the club members.

"Nothing," Cathleen said hesitantly, "but in a couple of weeks —"

"A couple of weeks is no good!" In a couple of weeks the election would be over. To get her picture on the front page of the local paper next week, she would need a fat check to hand over to a UNICEF representative by Saturday, Sunday at the latest. "Cathleen, I've got to go."

"But —"

Vanessa hung up. The problem was obvious. Her club members weren't inspired to collect donations, and the reason was because they weren't getting paid for it. Sympathy for unknown hungry children was not strong enough motivation for a bunch of spoiled teenagers to pound the pavement. She needed to *hire* people to solicit money. In fact, she could use a percentage of the donations to pay salaries. Legally — she knew from her mother's charity work — that was an acceptable practice, as long as the organization was recognized as nonprofit and receipts were given to the contributors. The only problem was the opinion of the other kids at school. They might feel she was reneging on her "own efforts" pledge. The only way to get around that would be to hire people from out of town. But how could she organize a second group large enough to gather the kind of money she needed in the time she had left?

Lightning struck, inside as well as outside. She didn't wait to hear the thunder before digging out the telephone directory for the adjacent town. She remembered seeing a listing in the Yellow Pages concerning a teen job agency. They would have long lists of kids looking for work.

"It took only a minute to find the ad and dial the number. A young female voice answered. "Garrison's Teen Agency. This is Cindy Dryer. May I help you?"

"Yes, my name is Vanessa Barlow. What time are you open till today?"

"Six o'clock. Are you an unemployed teen looking for work, Vanessa?"

Garrison was not too far. She could make it if she hurried. "No, I'm an employer," she said.

The phosphorescent hands on Nancy's watch were both pointing to three. She hadn't been up this late in years. Strange how she didn't feel tired. It must be the rain, the excitement, Alex.

The Clinton had been a repulsively rowdy, smoke-filled club, but the band — The Stray Leopards — had been a knock-out, incredibly tight for a new group, supporting Alex's high and melodious voice admirably. Like his dancing, his singing relied more upon style than unadulterated ability. She wasn't complaining; she believed he would go far . . . as long as he didn't run into her father tonight. Less than a mile left to go to her house, and Alex's twice rebuilt Mustang was showing no sign of collapsing. He would probably expect her to invite him in. Little did he know that a few minutes hence she planned on climbing in Olivia's back window and spending the rest of the night there.

"Next week, I'm going to try inviting some other people from school," Alex said, still riding a high from his performance. "If they dress maturely, I doubt the owner would ask for ID."

"What's the matter?" she joked. "You didn't like your Tarenton High audience tonight?"

He downshifted, easing the car around a flooded corner. The storm was showing no let up. "Not at all. I loved how you screamed my name after every song."

"I did *no* such thing." She had sat silently at the back of the club, hoping no one from school would show up. Regrettably, Steve Dextrile — Vanessa's boyfriend and team quarterback — had stumbled in during the last hour. She didn't believe he had seen her, if in fact he had still been able to see at all . . . yet she was not sure.

"Must have been one of my many unknown fans," he kidded. She poked him.

"Get out of here! I'm the *only* fan you've got." The words were out of her mouth before she realized how much they revealed. Alex didn't miss the admission.

"I wouldn't mind if you were," he said seriously.

"What do you mean?" She *had* to ask, had to have something concrete to support her round-the-clock fantasies.

"Just what I said. I don't need a huge crowd of screaming groupies. If I performed to a hall that had only one person in the seats that I cared about, that would be enough for me."

He was talking about her. "What a beautiful thing to say." She realized how, after the pain and humiliation Rick had caused her, she needed someone like Alex.

He grinned. "And as soon as I find that person, I'll quit inviting my groupies backstage."

"You conceited . . . !" she yelled, drawing her fist back for a playful punch. Then she froze. He reached the front of her house. Her parents would hear the Mustang stopping. "Keep driving," she said.

"Has your family moved in the last few hours?"

How he knew where she lived in the first place, since he had picked her up at school, was a good question. But it was not pressing. "No . . . I'm spending the night with Olivia."

"I see," he nodded, not needing many clues to catch the whole picture. "So your parents didn't know you were going out tonight?"

"They did!"

"With Olivia? Come on, Nancy. Was it the late hour, or that we were going to a club, or that I'm in a new wave band, or that I wear a gold earring?" He bypassed her house, turning left at the next street. His tone was difficult to read. She didn't want to hurt his feelings with the truth, and ruin the night. But she was a rotten liar.

She touched his arm. "I'm sorry, Alex, it's not that I'm ashamed of you," she said softly.

He did not answer, slowing for another flooded area, making another left, going in circles. They would run out of gas next. The silence was hard on her, draining her own reserves. "Head for the school," she said finally, "and please talk to me."

"I'm thinking," he said softly.

"Tell me."

"Whether it would help the situation if I wore my earring on the left ear."

"You're impossible," she growled while he laughed. Still, his humor was a relief. She had half expected him to respond angrily. She didn't know if she could have handled that. Apparently she didn't *really* know him, as she had pretended she did.

"Why are we going to the school?" he asked, still chuckling.

"We can park in the lot and talk. I'm trying to tell you something."

His demeanor changed. When he wanted to, he could be serious. "I think I understand the situation. If I want to see you, it seems I will have to alter my image."

"I don't want you to." She shook her head,

suddenly embarrassed that he presumed so much. "What I'm asking is, "Why should you *want* to bother?"

The school was not far from her house. He eased over the speed bumps on the parking lot ramp and swung into the principal's reserved spot, turning off the engine. The patter of rain drops on the car roof was lulling. More than anything, she wanted to curl up and spend the rest of the night in his arms.

"I'll have to think about it," he said quietly, staring straight out the window at the dark buildings. "Not because you might not be worth it — you're more important than the sacrifice of a piece of jewelry and a hairstyle — but because who I am is a lot more than the way I look. If your parents don't like me in my usual clothes, I doubt they would like me in a dark blue suit with a red tie."

His confession of his feelings for her added a dreamlike quality to the night, while at the same time making the situation all that more gloomy. "A change in dress would at least give them a chance to know you," she said.

He leaned his head on the steering wheel, turning toward her, reaching out his hand and touching her knee beneath the hem of her dress. "Are you sure?"

"No."

"I didn't think so." He smiled — a drowsy smile, a sexy smile. He took her arm and gently pulled her toward him, the feeling not unlike slipping into a warm bath. She wrapped her arms around his chest, pressing her head against his shirt, listening to his heart beat. His fingers slipped through her hair, taunting nerves deep in her scalp, the sensation both relaxing and unmistakably exciting. "Should we do it?" he asked casually.

She gulped, not sure what he meant. Better to play it safe. "Do *what*?"

"Kiss," he said, laughing.

He was as nervous as she was, the faker. His heartbeat had doubled with her "Do what?" She looked up at him. "You can do better than that, Alex."

"I can?" he smiled nervously.

It was fun turning the tables on him, especially since she didn't have that much experience making out. She sat up, lightly kissed his chin, his cheek, his nose. He watched her with nothing short of amazement.

"Have you gone to sleep, or what?" she asked.

He hadn't. Alex did everything with style. And Nancy responded to him with joy. Joy at being with someone open and honest and loving. She blocked her father's angry face out, as she kissed Alex with longing. He was aware of her longing and his own, but he didn't push her further than she wanted to go.

On Monday, they had the whole gym to themselves. Even Mrs. Engborg, held up in a faculty meeting, was not present. They should have been using the time wisely instead of listening to Nancy's ravings about how they had to incorporate Alex's suggestions into their routine. Mary Ellen thought it was just a delayed reaction to her frustration at not being selected for the homecoming queen court. Nancy was trying to distract herself with a cause.

"We have to be realistic," Nancy was saying, pacing across the maple floor in front of the stands where the rest of them were gathered in a haphazard fashion. Walt was halfway up the bleachers, spinning a basketball on the tip of his finger. Pres was a couple of rows beneath him, browsing through a magazine. Olivia sat at Pres's feet, looking her usual cool self. Angie was leaning against the far wall.

"If we tighten our transitions," Nancy continued, "clap our hands louder and bounce an extra inch higher, the best we can do is add one or two points to our score."

"Two points more *would* have tied us for first," Mary Ellen said, content to wait out this silly notion with calm logic.

"In the prelim, yes," Nancy said. "This Saturday, our competition will be much stiffer. We need to be more exciting."

"I could wear my see-through uniform," Angie muttered, watching Walt spin the ball.

"I could dig out my Elton John sunglasses," Walt added.

"I'm serious," Nancy said, sounding awfully serious.

"If you're so serious," Mary Ellen said, "why did you wait till now to bring it up? You know we have a big five days left."

"Isn't it obvious? I wanted to see how we would do in the prelims with what we had."

"We're arguing about nothing," Mary Ellen

said. "How do we know Alex can teach us anything worthwhile? Sure, I saw him dance, and he's no slouch, but that doesn't mean he knows what the judges want. Take Weston High, for example. They scored the fifty-one and I didn't see anything new wave in their routine."

"I did," Pres said quietly, laying aside his magazine. "They did a lot more with their hips, and their hands were very suggestive in their movements."

"They also used Billy Idol's music," Olivia said.

Nancy was gaining confidence. "Give Alex a chance to see what he can teach us. That's all I'm asking. I can call him right now and he'll be here in fifteen minutes."

"I wish I had a boyfriend like that," Angie said, tiring of her game, standing and stretching. "I call Marc and leave a message and get a third class postcard from him a month later."

"Let's take a vote," Pres said, casting a brief glance at Mary Ellen to gauge her reaction to the suggestion. She had on her poker face. "I, personally, am in favor of seeing what Alex has to offer."

Pres had called Sunday — yesterday — to see how she was. But it had been Patrick who had actually come over. She compared the two in every way. Pres was rich and smooth. But Patrick excited her. Yet Pres's money, his position, excited her in a totally different way. Chances were they would both end up hating her and she would have nothing to worry about.

"So am I," Olivia said, breaking into Mary Ellen's thoughts.

"I'll let him in the gym, if he lets me try on his earring," Walt laughed, setting down his basketball.

"Angie?" Nancy asked.

Angie shrugged. "As long as he doesn't charge us anything."

"Seems I'm outvoted," Mary Ellen mused, knowing she still held all the cards.

"Will you tell Mrs. Engborg that we'd like Alex's help?" Nancy asked.

"Tell her yourself," Mary Ellen said. "She'll be here in a few minutes."

Nancy tried not to let her anger show. She would make a lousy actress. "The first thing she'll ask is if we are all in agreement. If I say no, she'll tell me to forget it." Nancy took a quick breath. "As squad captain, you should speak for the group."

Mary Ellen could feel herself being dragged into an argument. "As squad captain, I have the right to recommend what I think is best."

Nancy tossed aside all attempt to hide her animosity. "Why are you opposing Alex's help? Or is it that you're just opposing *me*?"

Mary Ellen had been pleased at how calmly she had been dealing with the situation. Now she began to have doubts. *Was* she resisting because it was Nancy's idea? No . . . there simply wasn't time left to change their routine. As much to reassure herself as to convince Nancy, she said, "This is *not* a personality contest."

Nancy laughed without mirth. "Everything with you is a personality contest, your ego's so big."

"I thought I had the biggest one," Walt said, nervously. He wanted to avoid a fight between Nancy and Mary Ellen at all costs.

"Yours is heavier," Angie said. "Mary Ellen's is bigger."

Mary Ellen was mad now and she had absolutely no doubt about that. "*My* ego's big? Who thinks she's so hot that she has a boyfriend who can talk to us for five minutes and turn us into superstars?"

"Girls . . ." Pres began.

Nancy stopped pacing and jammed her fists against her hips. "Of course *you* don't need Alex! You're already a superstar! You're a legend in your own mind — you're such a . . . *pretty princess*!"

"Hey, go easy on the pretty princesses," Angie said.

"As to *your* Alex and his earring, what do you see in him, anyway?"

"A lot more than I see in your garbage man!" Nancy yelled.

"He's not a garbage man!" she yelled back.

"Stop it!" Olivia shouted.

They stopped it. Mary Ellen discovered that she was standing and sat back down. Nancy walked ten yards and also sat down. The reason the command had been so effective was because it had come from Olivia. As far as any of them knew, Olivia had never shouted in her life, except once at her mother. It had been a shock. Even Olivia herself looked a bit shocked. Pres took the floor.

"I think both of you should apologize," he said.

"I'm sorry that Alex dresses peculiarly," Mary Ellen grumbled.

"And I'm sorry that Patrick drives a garbage truck and that Mary Ellen is a snob," Nancy replied, staring at the floor.

Walt rubbed his eyes, sighing loudly, "It always chokes me up to see two fine people reconcile their differences."

Mary Ellen was not sure who started laughing first. It was probably Angie, possibly Nancy, maybe even herself. How or where it began was not important, because it was instantly contagious. The shouting match had been funny, and since they had scored evenly, it left no hard feelings.

When Mrs. Engborg arrived five minutes later, they were still laughing.

Alex's help was not mentioned again during practice. Going through their four sections, feeling a vague boredom with their entire routine, Mary Ellen began to wonder if *she* shouldn't give him a call.

CHAPTER

Vanessa Barlow was not sure she had heard correctly. Whenever Steve Dextrile spoke more than three consecutive sentences, she had a habit of tuning him out. As they were in the school library, where frivolous talk was not permitted, she had been particularly deaf and discouraging to Steve's long-winded monologues. But a name he had dropped stood out in sharp relief.

"*Who* did you see at the Clinton?" she asked, closing her geometry book.

Steve also set aside his book. "They got *down*, let me tell you. Their singer, that Alex dude —"

"I don't care about the band," she interrupted. "Did you say you saw Nancy Goldstein at the club?"

Steve nodded. "Yeah, she probably came to see Alex sing. I've seen them holding hands at lunch. That guy's got a great voice. He. . . ."

Vanessa again blotted him out. She knew

Nancy's parents. They wouldn't have let their daughter go to a rowdy club thirty miles away. Nancy must have done it without their knowing. Naturally, she wouldn't have wanted anyone to know she was in a joint that served liquor. That alone was grounds enough to be expelled from the squad.

Vanessa decided the time had come to modify her plans. A couple of hours ago at lunch, Mary Ellen had approached her and had said, wearing a smug expression, that there was no need to worry about the money. That could only mean someone was giving her the five hundred dollars, her parents or Pres — probably Pres. She could see it now — Mary Ellen running weeping to rich Pres and telling him how wicked Vanessa Barlow had made her sign a devil's contract. It made Vanessa sick to think about it. Mary Ellen's need to quit the squad and get a job was apparently eliminated. She would be able to compete in this Saturday's state competition after all. If the squad won, they would have their pictures on the front page of next Wednesday's paper right before the homecoming queen election. And they *were* good, Vanessa had to admit. They could win. They had to be stopped.

"Steve," she interrupted whatever he was saying, "I want you to do me a favor." She smiled sweetly, touching his cheek. He sat up, straightening his bulky shoulders.

"Sure, Vanessa, anything you want."

"I want you to go see Mrs. Engborg right now and tell her that you saw Nancy Goldstein at the Clinton Saturday night."

He looked worried, confused. "That could get her in trouble. Cheerleaders aren't supposed to be in bars."

"Mrs. Engborg should learn that her girls are not the saints she thinks they are. Do this for me and I'll. . . ." She ran her fingers through his hair. ". . . I'll thank you kindly."

He did not leer like he usually did when she said something like that. If anything, he appeared more uncomfortable. "But football players aren't supposed to be in bars, either. If I tell Mrs. Engborg I saw Nancy, she'll know *I* was there, and she'll tell the coach."

She had been hoping he would overlook that possibility.

"I just don't want Coach to know I was drinking at a club. I like Nancy. I don't want to get her in trouble."

"Who do you like more, me or —"

"Shh!" Mrs. Guther, head librarian, scolded as she walked by, rapping her knuckles on their table. In a place where she couldn't yell at him, Vanessa realized she'd get nowhere with Steve. Through the library windows, she could see Cathleen Eismar walking across the courtyard. Gathering up her books, kissing Steve's cheek, and telling him to forget the whole thing, she hurried out the door to catch up to Cathleen in the parking lot. Vanessa didn't waste time with small talk. She got down to business, explaining Steve's spotting Nancy at the club and his refusal to tell Mrs. Engborg.

"It's understandable that he wouldn't want to put himself on the spot," Cathleen said.

Vanessa shrugged. "If he's so worried about what his coach thinks, why does he get loaded at joints like the Clinton?"

"I thought you liked Steve."

"Look, I'm not here to talk about Steve or Mary Ellen. I want Nancy off the squad. When you get home, call her house and ask for her. Nancy will still be at practice. When her mother tells you this, ask if Alex will be coming by the house later. Immediately, Mrs. Goldstein will want to know who Alex is. Act surprised, like you assumed everyone *knew* Nancy was dating Alex. Mention the way he dresses, how he sings in a new wave band, where he plays. Don't state specifically that Nancy was at the Clinton Saturday night. Let Mrs. Goldstein figure that out for herself. When Nancy gets home, her dad will ground her. Cheerleading practice will go right out the window. Don't forget, even more so than Mary Ellen, Nancy was responsible for stealing *your* position on the cheerleading squad. You owe her one."

The reminder sunk in, causing a wave of resentment. "I'll call her mother when I get home," Cathleen said with determination.

Olivia Evans found Coach Riley at the stadium track, timing the cross-country team in quarter-mile intervals. With the recent rain, the orange-red cinders were soaked. The team was running barefoot on the grass, inside lane one. Michael was not there.

"Hello, Olivia," Coach Riley said. "What can I do for you today?"

Olivia watched as the front runners rounded the nearest curve. She had exactly 330 yards worth of time to talk to the coach before the runners returned.

"I know that the cross-country meet is scheduled against Wickfield for Saturday evening during halftime."

"Yeah, not that I like it," he said, consulting one of the numerous stopwatches hanging from his neck. Olivia wondered if he heard ticking when he was trying to fall asleep at night. "That's homecoming night and I imagine halftime is going to be busy. They have to crown the new queen and all. Another time would have been better."

"The crowning ceremony will easily fit between the start and finish of the race," Olivia said.

She had to get to what she'd wanted to talk to the coach about quickly. He would undoubtedly reassure her.

"Coach, once you mentioned that Wickfield had an exceptional runner. I was wondering . . . could Michael lose to him? I wouldn't want that to happen in front of so many people."

Coach Riley did not laugh like she had been hoping. "Michael stepped on a piece of glass while running barefoot on the grass here Monday morning," he said sadly. "He hasn't been back to school since. Knowing him, I bet he can't stand the thought of anyone seeing him on crutches."

Olivia was horrified. "Is it bad?"

"Fifteen stitches, but it'll heal. Still, I doubt he'll be ready for the Wickfield meet. Even if he did run, against David Clare he wouldn't do very well. That kid's strong and Michael will have lost his edge."

Olivia almost groaned out loud. The little she knew of Michael told her he would try to run.

Nancy Goldstein knew she was in trouble the instant she saw her father's face. For one thing, it was four o'clock, and he usually didn't get home till six. He was usually a contained man, and didn't go around looking like someone had just died. As she passed beneath his frozen grey eyes and set her books on a living room table, she had the strong feeling that she was in trouble.

"Your mother spoke with Olivia's mother a little while ago," he said softly.

Nancy wondered where her mother was . . . wished she was present. Her mother was the pacifier in the house. No doubt that was why her father had asked to talk to Nancy alone.

"Oh," she said, turning away, knowing pretense was pointless but willing to give it a try. "What did she have to say?"

She heard her father move a step closer to her back. "She said you did *not* stay over Saturday night."

Nancy took a deep breath, fighting to stay calm. The tears forming in her eyes made it hard to pretend. "That's not true," she whispered.

David Goldstein came a step closer. "Where were you Saturday night?" he asked in the same soft voice. "With some boy named *Alex*?"

Nancy felt her feeble reserve crumble. She nodded. "Part of the night, yes, but only part of the night." How had he found out?

He took hold of her arm and turned her around. It was not a yank nor, when they were face-to-face, was he preparing to yell at her. He didn't even look that angry. But the disappointment in his austere face cut deeper than any rage could have. "Why did you lie to your mother and me?"

She was trembling. "I wanted to go out with him. I wanted to —"

"What were you doing with that boy all night?" he interrupted quietly, firmly.

"It *wasn't* all night," she wept. "He plays in a band and I just wanted to hear him play."

"I *know* what he does," he said, raising his voice, picking up a trace of disgust. "Your friend Cathleen called and accidentally informed your mother. He's one of those punk rockers who break things and have tramps for girl friends."

That he could say such a thing to her hurt Nancy more than she could have imagined. The pain was so sharp, she couldn't even absorb it. She felt a sudden numbness deep inside, like a part of her had ceased to exist. She couldn't speak for a moment.

Then she found her voice. "Dad, please listen. Alex is not what you think. He's nice and kind and . . . and you'd like him. I know it."

"I doubt that very much," her father said. "Very much."

Mr. Goldstein pointed to the hallway. "Go to your room and stay there until dinner. There is to be no more going out at night; no more parties; and no more cheerleading. You are finished for this year, Nancy. And if that friend of yours should ever show his face around here, he will dearly regret it. Is that understood?"

Unable to fight him any longer, Nancy stumbled down the hall, and shut herself in her bedroom. Her phone was on her pillow. She had to make one call. The number was on a slip of paper in her sweater pocket. She dialed with trembling fingers and Alex's mother answered.

"Hello?"

"Hello, Mrs. Hague? Is Alex there?"

"No, he's not. He's practicing with his band. Is this Nancy?"

Nancy had called before and the first two times she had also talked to his mother. "Yes."

"You sound awful. Is something wrong?"

"No, nothing's wrong. . . . When will he be home?"

"I'd say in about an hour. Would you like me to have him call you?"

Her number was unlisted. As a precaution, she had not given it to Alex, trying to protect herself as much as possible. Alex had not liked it, but he tried to understand her anxiety. Now she was glad for her cautiousness. "No. I'll call him back."

"Are you sure you're all right?"

"I'm fine, just fine. Thank you, Mrs. Hague." She set down the phone and lay back on her bed, staring at the ceiling. In the months to come, she would probably learn every detail of the ceiling perfectly. She didn't know what was causing her the most pain, not being able to see Alex or not being on the squad. *The squad,* she thought, almost breaking apart with concern. What would happen to them? Who would take her place? She knew her father too well to think he would change his mind, and she didn't have the strength to fight him. Someone else might, but she didn't.

Vanessa Barlow set down the phone. She had just spoken to Cindy Dryer at the Garrison Teen Agency. All was going well with the hiring of kids to collect tax deductible donations for Food for the Forgotten. Saturday, she had given Cindy the necessary receipts and pamphlets. This latest call had been to emphasize the importance of this first week's collection. Vanessa smiled to herself.

Then Vanessa flipped open her little black book and checked under the K's for Mary Ellen Kirkwood. Mary Ellen answered after the first ring.

"Hello?"

"Hi, honey. Guess who this is?" Vanessa asked, coyly.

"What do you want?"

"How rude you are!"

"I told you this afternoon you'd get your money. That's all I have to say. Now if you'll excuse me, I'm going —"

"Don't hang up," Vanessa cut in. "I have something *I* want to say. Tarenton High's cheerleading squad will not be competing in this Saturday's state finals."

Mary Ellen paused. "Really? Who's going to stop us?"

"*Nancy* and you. As of this moment, Nancy is grounded for being out late in the company of a questionable young man. Feel free to call her to check out the accuracy of this information."

"I will. What's going to stop *me,* or need I ask?"

Vanessa laughed. "You're going to be sick this Saturday, as sick as you were a couple of weeks ago. If not, copies of a certain I.O.U. will find their way into circulation Monday morning at school. I don't have to remind you how incriminating those copies can be. You were drunk, you know."

Mary Ellen thought for a minute. "How do I know copies of the I.O.U. won't be circulated no matter what I do?" she asked desperately.

"You'll have to trust me!" Vanessa did not even try to suppress the glee in her voice.

"That'll be the day. By the way, do you have any shiny poisonous apples you want me to taste?" She tried to be funny, to hide her fear from Vanessa.

"Of course I won't let anyone know about the I.O.U., until I get all my money," Vanessa lied. "Not unless you push me."

"If Nancy is out, why are you hassling me? With even one member absent, we can't perform."

"I believe there is safety in numbers. Two is better than one."

"Who do you expect to fool? I know you and Cathleen conspired to get me drunk at the party."

Vanessa was not surprised Mary Ellen had figured that out. The girl was no dummy. "I can't wait to see you try and explain *that* to the whole student body."

"I won't try," Mary Ellen said, sounding suddenly weary. "If Nancy won't be coming, there is no reason why I shouldn't call in sick." She felt as if her life was falling apart and she couldn't figure out how to save it. And Nancy, poor Nancy. Her father must be furious.

"You always were reasonable. Now that our business is complete, I'll let you go," Vanessa said.

"Wonderful," Mary Ellen answered. "But there is one thing you should know. No matter what you do — your phony clubs, your blackmail threats, your smear campaigns — you won't be elected queen. When a monster dresses in silk, it's still a monster."

Vanessa glared at the sudden silent phone. Mary Ellen had hung up on her.

Slamming down the receiver in Vanessa's ear, Mary Ellen almost fell out of her chair with the wave of despair that hit her. Vanessa had her cornered, had *all* of them trapped. There would be no state championship this year, no homecoming nomination this time. . . .

Coward, she thought, you're giving up without a fight.

So she didn't know what to do — but someone else might. Wasn't she big enough to admit when she needed help? And there was one person with whom help might be a two-way street. A couple of hours ago the two of them had been going at it like cats and dogs, but if Vanessa really had put the fix on Nancy, then there could be no one in the world more likely to understand *her* predicament. They were teammates, after all. Mary Ellen picked up the phone and dialed Nancy's number.

"Hello?" Nancy answered weakly.

"Nancy, is that you? It's Mary Ellen."

"Is it?"

Nancy sounded *terrible*. It strengthened Mary Ellen's resolve that they could not sit back and be manipulated. "Listen, Nancy, I want to hold a meeting of the whole squad right now."

"No meeting," Nancy mumbled. "Grounded . . . can't come."

"I know. Vanessa told me."

Nancy showed signs of life. "*Vanessa* told you?"

"I'll explain when I see you. I'm going to call the others. If you can't leave the house, we'll come to you. I don't know exactly what's happened to you, but believe me, you're not alone."

Nancy was interested. "Don't go to my front door. Cut through the field in back. I'll have my bedroom window wide open. Be very quiet."

"Good. We'll be there soon. Keep up your spirits."

Nancy gave a sad chuckle. "That's what I'm supposed to be an expert at, isn't it?"

CHAPTER

Although their meeting had brought about no solution so far, Nancy felt new strength in her friends' company. Sitting atop her pillows, huddled in a blanket, she glanced at the clock beside her bed. It was eight o'clock. She had told her parents she didn't want dinner. Never mind that the squad had been talking in whispers — it was a small miracle her mom and dad hadn't heard them. She was not worried what they would do if they *did* walk in. Her punishment couldn't get any worse.

"This is better than *Dynasty* and *Dallas* put together," Angie said as Mary Ellen finished a detailed account of what had happened to her at Vanessa's party.

"How can you say *better*?" Mary Ellen asked, annoyed. "It hurts you as much as it hurts me."

"But it does have its amusing side," Angie said. Mary Ellen scowled.

"Notice how Cathleen was involved in what happened to Nancy and Mary Ellen," Pres said, sitting against the far wall next to Mary Ellen. "She must be in cahoots with Vanessa. But Vanessa is undoubtedly the instigator. It's her we have to get back at." He frowned. "We just need a hook to catch her with."

They reviewed Vanessa Barlow's history. Though filled with atrocities, none had occurred since she had supposedly "felt a strong need to help humanity." Finally they latched onto her club as the best way to get at her. But in what way? It appeared another dead end until Mary Ellen jumped to her feet and began to pace.

"We know Vanessa founded the club to improve her image. She wants to present a large check to someone important and get her picture in the paper. She implied as much at the party. To do her any good in the homecoming queen standings, she'll have to do this by next Saturday. Walt, you mentioned how you heard she agreed to match dollar for dollar the donations her club members gathered. Where is *she* getting the money?"

Pres shrugged. "Probably her parents."

Nancy shook her head. "Dr. and Mrs. Barlow are tight. Take my word for it. My mother went shopping with Mrs. Barlow a few times when we first moved here from Ohio and that woman wanted my mother to chip in for gas."

"She could be raising it from businesses," Walt said.

Mary Ellen shook her head. "Still, it makes no sense. There would have to be two dozen of her going door-to-door to match all the club members' donations."

"She probably hired people in other places to collect the money," Angie muttered, getting bored with all the talk and looking around for something to eat.

"Maybe that's it!" Mary Ellen exclaimed.

"Shh!!" Nancy hissed, holding her breath in wait for her parents. Yet, it was weird — neither of her parents appeared. Why? Were they never going to speak to her again? This analysis was all well and good for solving Mary Ellen's predicament, but Nancy felt like Dorothy in the *Wizard of Oz* must have, when she first realized there was nothing in the wizard's magic bag to help her get home. Nancy wanted to go home — to the way home had been yesterday.

"That's got to be it," Mary Ellen repeated in an excited whisper. "And I bet she's using a good chunk of the money collcted to cover salaries. Angie, you're a genius."

"Ain't it the truth," Angie said. "Are we done? Let's go to McDonald's."

"How would she know enough people in another part of the county?" Walt asked.

"Maybe she's using an employment agency," Pres said. "I would if I were in her situation. Vanessa is a master at delegating responsibility."

"You mean, she's lazy," Mary Ellen said. "But I hope you're right. It would make it that much easier to track down her help."

"This is my department," Walt said, reaching for the phone. "I'll call Steve Dextrile and terrify him about his drinking at the Clinton. He'll tell me whether Vanessa has been making any trips to other cities. If we get a town, I'll call their chamber of commerce and get a list of every local employment agency."

While Walt went about his investigating, Mary Ellen came and sat beside Nancy on the bed, hugging her with one arm. Nancy hugged her back. She had never thought she would feel close to Mary Ellen, but she did now. It was strange how it had taken the possible breakup of the squad to make them feel like part of the same group.

"You're worried that your parents are going to be mad at you forever, aren't you, Nancy?" Mary Ellen said softly.

She nodded, whispering, "And I'm afraid I won't be able to see Alex anymore. That's . . . that hurts, you know?"

"This will not last," Mary Ellen said firmly, squeezing her shoulder. "*We* won't let it. Your parents love you. When they hear the whole truth, they'll apologize for being so harsh."

"I hope so," she said, though she could not imagine it.

Mary Ellen took her hand. "Another thing, if we get the chance, I want to use Alex's help."

Nancy didn't know what to say. Who was this stranger trying to comfort her? They were so often thrown together in competitive situations that it was easy to forget that having similar goals did not mean that they had to fight each other to reach them. Tarenton was big enough for the both of them.

"This whole thing has made me realize we

have to stick together," Mary Ellen continued. "I'm sure Alex could . . . darn you, Angie! What are you laughing at?"

Trying to bury her giggles in the corner of the sheet, Angie gasped, "It's too rich, seeing the two of you sweet talking each other!"

The moment was lost. Turning a deep red, Mary Ellen withdrew her hand and sat glaring at Angie. Nancy didn't mind. Mary Ellen had revealed something new — compassion. They were friends at the moment, even if they returned to being enemies later on.

Walt, a masterful actor on the phone, politely threatened to tell the coach and every college in the country that offered football scholarships about a certain someone's boozing binge, and had Steve Dextrile trembling in his sneakers. It didn't take long to learn that Vanessa had run out to Garrison at least once in the last week. Unfortunately, they soon discovered that most of that town's employment agencies were already closed. Going down a list provided by telephone information — Garrison's Chamber of Commerce was also closed — Walt was about to give up when he got an answer at a teenage agency.

"Hello, this is Fredrick Kirkpatrick," Walt said, sounding twice his age. "I'm a member of the faculty at Tarenton High. I am not sure if I have the right number, so please correct me if I'm wrong. Are you the agency that is currently helping Vanessa Barlow collect donations for a UNICEF club?" Walt sucked in a breath, put his hand over the receiver, and nodded excitedly. Walt continued calmly, "Excellent. Vanessa gave me your number but I was afraid that I had copied it down incorrectly. The reason I'm calling, Cindy, is that the teachers at Tarenton High wanted to send a personal thank-you note to each youngster who is helping Vanessa in her good work. . . . Yes, I understand the kids are already being paid, as they should be. But we wanted to do a little something extra for them. . . . You have a list of their names and addresses on your desk? Wonderful." Pres handed Walt a pen and paper. ". . . Yes, I'm ready. You can give me the information. . . ."

Ten minutes later Walt was off the phone and receiving hearty congratulations, particularly from Mary Ellen, who gave him a bear hug and a kiss on the lips. "Walt, I adore you!" she exclaimed.

"I only wish Vanessa got you in hot water more often," Walt said, obviously savoring the affection. He caught Pres's eye, giving him a wink. Pres slapped him on the back. Mary Ellen snatched up the list of Vanessa's employees and held the paper as though it were made of gold.

"I'm going to wait until that witch commits herself to the newspapers," she said. "After she goes on record with a reporter that she *personally* raised the money, I'll hit her with this list." Mary Ellen was going to burst with joy. "I'll have her right where I want her — kissing my feet!"

Pres pulled the list from Mary Ellen's fingers, folded it carefully, and put it in his back pocket. "Nothing will be gained by humiliating her," he warned. "We'll get the I.O.U. back in exchange for these names and call it even."

"*What?*" Mary Ellen said.

"Justice, not revenge," Angie said philosophically. "Can we eat?"

"Let's not stoop to Vanessa's level," Pres said.

"Okay," Mary Ellen agreed reluctantly. "But we're making copies of that list, just in case."

Despite her own troubles, Nancy truly was happy for Mary Ellen. But it was time the party ended. "You guys better split out the window," she said. "With all the commotion we've been making, we've been lucky my parents haven't already broken down the door."

Mary Ellen shook her head. "We're not sneaking out of here. We're going to talk to your parents and explain that they are being unreasonable."

"But. . . . ?"

"Don't worry, it's our rear ends," Walt said.

"It's your *lives*," Nancy said. They didn't understand that her dad's mind was harder to change than Earth's direction around the sun. Her pleading did nothing to dissuade them, the foolish martyrs. Mary Ellen opened the bedroom door and the group headed down the hall. Nancy had no choice but to follow.

Mozart, she thought. Since when did Dad play like that?

Before she reached the living room, she knew the musician at the piano could not possibly be her father. This person was an accomplished artist, not someone who had decided a year ago that he'd like to learn an instrument.

Dressed in bright red pants, a starched white shirt, and a black bow tie, not to mention his gold earring, Alex was sitting at the piano, concentrating on sheets of music her father was carefully turning. Nancy's mother was sitting on the couch, her eyes half closed, wearing a faint smile. The entrance of their entire squad caused hardly a ripple. Her father glanced up but that was all. No one spoke until Alex had finished his piece.

"What's going on here?" Mary Ellen asked, incredulously.

Alex looked up at Nancy's father, who said, "We've been enjoying a classical concert." His hand dropped to Alex's shoulder and squeezed it. Nancy wondered if she wasn't actually asleep on her bed and dreaming. "Are you getting tired, son?"

Alex nodded. "A bit. We'll have to play together another time."

Her father laughed. "I think it would be better if I did more listening than playing. But I wouldn't mind another lesson. You taught me more this evening than I've learned in the last year."

"I loved that last piece," her mother said dreamily. "It made me feel like I was floating."

Alex smiled. "Mozart can do that."

The universal language, Nancy thought. Alex hadn't tried to win her parents with words. He had used music. How he had got past the front door to the piano was a question that could wait. A weight she had feared she would have to carry a long time was instantly lifted. Like her mother, she could have floated away.

"My mother told me you called, Nancy," Alex explained. "Since I didn't have your number and it wasn't listed, I thought I'd stop by. Your folks and I discovered we both love classical music. We've been playing and talking Mozart and Bach for the last two hours. We were just about to go get you."

"We were reluctant to interrupt your party," her father said, a hint of seriousness returning.

"It was a surprise party," Mary Ellen said, pulling up a foot stool and sitting down. "Nancy didn't know we were coming."

"It was a going away party," Angie said cheerfully. "We heard that you two, Mr. and Mrs. Goldstein, were going to kill her."

Whatever last traces of tension existed were washed away as they all laughed together. Nancy did not remember crossing the room but she found herself in her father's arms, hugging him tightly. Though notoriously shy in public, he returned her embrace.

"I'm still angry at you," he said gently when she let go. "I'm sorry, Nancy, I really was wrong about you and Alex. But you should have told us about him. You should have brought him here so we could talk to him, get to know him. We aren't monsters, you know." Mr. Goldstein kissed Nancy's cheek.

"I was afraid," she said honestly.

"Of what?" her mother asked.

Alex winked at her. "She didn't think you'd like my earring," Alex said, playing with the gold band.

Her father grinned, caught himself, and frowned. "Do you have to wear it even when you're not on stage?"

"To tell you the truth, I don't know how to take it off."

More laughter. It *was* turning into a party. Mary Ellen took advantage of the gaiety to ask, "Mr. Goldstein? Could you please wait until next week after the state finals to punish Nancy?"

Her father smiled. "Now that we have a better understanding of one another, I don't think punishment will be necessary."

"Are you quite sure, sir?" Walt asked seriously. "If you let these children run loose now, there is no telling how they'll —"

"Shut up!" Pres, Angie, Mary Ellen, Olivia, and Nancy said.

Walt smiled. "I was just joking."

"Hey, Alex," Mary Ellen added quickly, "how would you like to stop by our practice tomorrow and show us your fancy jungle moves?"

"What's wrong with now?" he asked.

Absolutely nothing. They worked on their routine till midnight. Once again, as they had been last spring working in the gym, they were a team . . . together . . . a dazzling unit sensing each other's movements almost before they were made.

CHAPTER

"Now smile as if Mr. Gerber were giving *you* the check for sixteen hundred dollars," the photographer, Al Scoly, said as he adjusted his Nikon camera atop its tripod.

Vanessa brushed aside her hair, flashed every one of her perfectly shiny teeth, and prominently displayed a check while grasping the UNICEF representative's outstretched hand. Mr. Gerber was in his nineties. His fingers trembled inside hers and she feared she might accidentally crack his brittle bones. She wasn't about to tell the old goat to take a hike, but she would have preferred a younger, more photogenic, man. The backdrop wasn't to her liking, either — Tarenton High's administration building. The picture should have been shot on the lake's pier, somewhere more exotic. On the other hand, given Mr. Gerber's unsteady nerves, he probably would have fallen in the water.

Al Scoly clicked off six shots and told them they could relax. Mr. Gerber put the check in his breast pocket, smiled at her with sad wrinkled eyes, climbed in the back of a chauffered limousine, and drove away. Earlier, a reporter had recorded her personal thoughts on how wonderful she was. Now that it was all over, she felt let down that a bigger deal hadn't been made of her contribution. Hoping that maybe that dark and blue-eyed Al Scoly would want to ask her out, she walked over to where he was dismantling his tripod.

"Do you have any more assignments today?" she asked brightly.

"Yeah, I've got to rush over to Chetfield."

For no reason she could immediately pinpoint, the town's name triggered an ominous feeling. "What's in Chetfield?"

Al slipped his camera in its case. "Don't you know? Your school's cheerleading squad is going out for the state championship today."

"That's off. One of the girls is sick and another has been temporarily dropped from the squad." She forced a smile. "It's a good thing I asked — saved you the trip."

Al shook his head. "I spoke on the phone with their coach not more than an hour ago. The entire squad was present and ready to compete."

Nancy and Mary Ellen had lied to her! Well, they would *pay*.

"May I go with you?" she asked.

"What?"

"I want to go with you to Chetfield."

Al nodded. "Fine with me."

* * *

In Chetfield Mary Ellen removed the cap from the liniment, squirted a larger than usual amount into her hands, and began to massage it into her calves. She was tight, and the heat helped relax her muscles. Getting out of Chetfield's gym had also helped. The place was a zoo, with twice the people they'd seen last Saturday. Contrary to Mrs. Engborg's orders, the friends and relatives of every member of the squad had made the drive down. Mary Ellen looked up from her seat on the sunlit bench. Gemma and Patrick huddled nervously three feet away.

"How do you feel?" Gemma asked.

"Like I need to stretch. How do I look?"

"Like a champ," Gemma said.

"That's my good luck charm," she smiled, lightly punching her sister. "I want you to do me a favor. Go tell Mrs. Engborg where I am and that I'll be back in a few minutes."

Gemma knew she was being told to leave. She didn't mind. Watching her go, Mary Ellen promised herself that she wouldn't disappoint Gemma. She patted the bench. "Come closer, Patrick. I'm glad you're here."

It never changed. When she was frightened, Patrick's presence gave her strength. He was the one she wanted to be near when she needed reassurance and bolstering. But coupled with that was the never ending attraction she felt for him. Her heart started to beat faster, her awareness of herself as a woman became stronger, and she felt that need to be held by him.

He leaned toward her and gently kissed her.

In spite of being visible, Mary Ellen put her arms around his neck and kissed him with all her heart and all her need.

"How *do* you feel," he asked, when she moved away from him, "besides wonderfully sexy?"

"Awful," she admitted. "And I don't suppose I look like a champ?"

He took her hand. "You always look great to me, you know."

He was trying to reassure, yet she couldn't miss hearing apprehension in his voice. "What is it?"

"Nothing, I'm just keeping my fingers crossed tight."

"For what?"

"For you to win, of course. What else?"

"Pres?" she asked. Patrick brushed aside the topic.

"We can talk about him later. I don't want to bother you now, not with all you've got on your mind."

"You know I'm seeing him? Well, sometimes."

Pat smiled. "I've known. Ahh . . . should I take back my ring?"

"You never gave me one."

He turned away. "I did buy you one."

Mary Ellen sighed to herself, looking straight up into the deep blue sky. Far above she saw a white bird floating on invisible wind currents. There were no boundaries to where it could go and for a moment she was envious, resenting the many complications in her life ready to hem her in. She pressed Patrick's hand between hers. "I like you, Patrick. I like Pres, too. Can I like you both and have neither of you hate me?"

Patrick didn't hesitate. "I don't have to own you."

Where would she ever again find such understanding? Never from Pres. She leaned forward to kiss Patrick again. It was then that she heard a familiar shout.

"Mary Ellen!" Mrs. Engborg called from the front door of the gym. "Get in here!"

In the gym, Nancy stared at the scoreboard and shook her head in disbelief. Five judges had given Gabriel High nines. One had awarded them a perfect score. That was fifty-five altogether, and to Nancy that was an unbeatable mark. "Incredible," was all she could say.

Alex pulled her off her seat on the bottom bleacher toward the lobby where the rest of the squad was gathering. "Look at it this way," he said. "The majority of judges thought there was still room for improvement."

Behind them, the speakers shouted, "*Tarenton High, ten minutes*!"

"Ten minutes," Nancy cringed. "I think the best we can hope for is second."

"That's a winner's attitude," Alex said sarcastically.

"But fifty-five, Alex — we can't beat that!"

"I'll be surprised if you don't get a perfect sixty. Haven't you had the greatest teacher? Come on, loosen up, you're here to have fun."

"I think I'd have more fun in front of a firing squad."

As they entered the lobby, they caught Mary Ellen and Patrick coming in from the outside.

Mary Ellen didn't have to ask. Nancy flashed two big fives. Their eyes rolled together. But like in her room on Monday, she felt strength in their being together. In the truest sense, they were totally dependent on one another.

"Just don't fall," Olivia's mother told her daughter. She turned to Mrs. Engborg, who sat on the identical chair she had last week, probably sipping her coffee out of the very same cup. "Is it absolutely necessary that they climb on top of each other at the end? That part always makes me nervous."

"They won't fall," Mrs. Engborg said flatly.

"But Olivia's not that strong, and sometimes she gets dizzy," Mrs. Evans said anxiously.

Olivia was firm. "I never get dizzy."

"Tell you what, Mrs. Evans," Walt said, bouncing up and down, either trying to charge up or dissipate his energy. "Olivia can take my place on the bottom."

While Mrs. Evans did her best to pretend she hadn't heard that remark, Angie did a practice cartwheel and accidentally took off the woman's hat. Fortunately, Marc caught it and handed it back with an apology for his girl friend's clumsy feet. Mary Ellen began to stretch in front of Pres and Patrick. Had circumstances been less tense, this triangle would have been interesting to watch. Olivia left her mother to continue her warm-up. Angie unwrapped a candy bar and threw away the chocolate instead of the wrapper. Nancy tried to blend into the wall, staring at her watch as though it were the center of the universe.

"*Tarenton High, five minutes*!" the speakers called.

Mrs. Engborg stood and, like last week, shook their hands and told them to simply do their best. Out of respect for Alex's contributions, which she had liked, she asked if he had any final words for the group.

"Go with the music," he said. "Pretend you're at a disco. I'll turn up the volume on the gym's amps. Knock them dead!"

This was it, Nancy thought, now and forever to the end of time. They would either be recognized as great or mediocre. In the middle of the group, head up, she strode through the doors and found her position on the floor. She couldn't see the crowd or the judges or the scoreboard. She didn't want to. She was alone with her friends, like in practice. It was no different. She took a deep breath and closed her eyes. The music began.

As it did, Al Scoly was running for the gym and Vanessa was chasing after him. He hoped to get pictures of the squad in action. *She* wanted to stop the squad. If she wasn't able to foil the cheerleaders, she could at least break Al's camera. There was no way Mary Ellen and company were going to replace her on the front page of Wednesday's paper.

She took her first step into the gym, where people were packed in like sardines, when the powerful opening chords of Michael Jackson's "Beat It!" ripped through the air. Momentarily thrown off balance, for she was out of breath and the music was loud, she didn't at first realize that it was Tarenton on the floor. What were they doing, shaking their arms like that? They looked like a bunch of break dancers.

"Great! What timing!" Al shouted, whipping out his camera and crouching with one knee on the hardwood floor, trying to get a shot between the pressed bodies. She shook his arm.

"That's not them!" she said. Jackson's voice screeched in her ears. "That's not Tarenton High!" she yelled.

He looked at her as if she were nuts. "What does that big red T on their shirts stand for!?"

"Tiremont!" she said, off the top of her head.

He waved her away. He hadn't been very friendly on the drive down. There wasn't much chance he was going to ask her out, especially if she cracked his five hundred dollar lens. She searched frantically for a fire alarm she could trip, a light switch she could short-circuit, anything that would stop them. But there was nothing, and she could only watch helplessly. Since when did Mary Ellen grab the end of her long hair and curl it between cartwheels? And the way Nancy was moving, it was . . .

"Obscene," she said.

"They're fantastic," Al agreed, snapping through his film at high speed.

To Pres, they were moving in soundless slow motion. It was a strange sensation. He had all the time in the world to direct the girls through their cartwheels. He was aware of the music, but it seemed he heard it through someone else's ears. He felt calm and in control.

This is a peak experience, he thought. I read about them last week in psychology.

Most of Alex's changes focused on the girls. The only alteration to Walt and his moves in the second section was the addition of a foot of lift to the girls' cartwheels. In practice this week Walt and he had had trouble adjusting quickly from Olivia to Angie, the two extremes of weight on the squad. Today he had no problem. He was on automatic pilot. He could relax and enjoy. It was a great show.

Olivia was flying through the air. Even as her feet slapped the floor, her head continued to soar, her thoughts a blur of movement and rhythm. The music, the twists, the jumps all blended into one beautiful whirling collage. She was dazzling . . . they were dazzling . . . everything was working.

They flowed into section three, the vault. With their change in song, the tempo had increased greatly, as had the complexity of their routines. Alex had introduced a spin and a throw of the head at their landings. After just a week of practice, the moves came spontaneously. Olivia no longer felt limited to her five-foot-long body. She was immersed in the group — laughing with Mary Ellen, clapping with Nancy, skipping with Angie, lifting with Walt and Pres. She couldn't make a mistake. She couldn't be afraid. It was impossible. She was having too much fun.

They climbed into their giant T. Normally they held it about ten seconds. But the standing ovation that erupted from the stands held them together over half a minute, long after the song was over. When Mary Ellen finally leaped off the top and curtsied at the microphone, the continuing applause drowned out her thank you. Incredibly, two judges left their seats to shake her hand.

What came next was like a dream. Olivia remembered walking to one end of the gym to wait for the score. Then the confusion began. People poured onto the floor, pressing tightly. Nancy was crying, Angie was laughing. Gemma was kissing Mary Ellen, and Walt and Pres were hugging each other. Nothing made sense, not even the fifty-six that flashed above in bright lights. There came another loud shout and cheerleaders Olivia didn't even know were shaking her hand and kissing her cheek. It was because they were the winners, she knew, but that didn't mean she had assimilated the fact. Only when Michael squeezed through the crowd and presented her with a bouquet of long stemmed roses did she wake from her trance and realize it was all true.

"You were sensational!" he said, giving her a quick hug. "I'm happy for you!"

"Thank you!" she called back over the din. No one had ever given her roses before. She didn't know what to say . . . how to feel. To her utter amazement, tears started to brim from her eyes. Quickly, she wiped them away. "How's your foot?"

"I had to give up football!"

"But you hate football!"

"So it was no problem!"

He was being silly and she decided it would

be all right to ask a dumb question. "Why are you here!?"

He smiled. He had such a nice smile, she wished he would show it more often. "To see you win!"

"But what if we had lost!?"

"Then I wouldn't have come!" He was having trouble keeping his position in the jostling crowd. "Do you need a ride home!?"

Somewhere in the swarming mass of people, she could hear her mother calling her name. It would be a drag trying to celebrate with her mother constantly checking her pulse. "Yes!" she said.

"You did it! You did it! You did it!" Gemma chanted.

"*I* didn't do it," Mary Ellen told her sister. "*We* all did it."

"Hey, does that include me?" Alex asked, coming over with an arm around a teary Nancy. Mary Ellen gave him a big hug.

"I can't thank you enough," she said, adding a kiss. Nancy playfully pushed her away.

"Don't worry," Nancy said. "He'll be adequately rewarded, by *me*." Then they laughed and embraced and Mary Ellen honestly felt Nancy and she would never fight again. At least not in the next week.

The judges were clearing the floor for the presentation of the trophy when Mary Ellen felt the insistent rapping on her shoulder. Turning, she found the icing on the cake, the thorn in her side — Vanessa.

"You can congratulate me later," Mary Ellen chuckled, showing Vanessa her back. But Vanessa was insistent and yanked her around.

"You're dead!" Vanessa said bitterly. "Come Monday there won't be a person down to the lowliest freshman that won't know you got stinking drunk at my party and broke my parents' vase. Your chum, Nancy, won't fare any better."

"But we're heroes," Mary Ellen said in mock amazement, pointing to the four-foot trophy that was being wheeled onto the floor. "See that bronze statue? They're going to put our name on it."

Vanessa sneered. "When the truth comes out, Tarenton High will be ashamed to engrave your name on it. You're a liar! You told me you weren't going to compete!"

"Excuse me," a dark, handsome, blue-eyed young man with a ton of photographic paraphernalia around his neck interrupted them. "My name is Al Scoly and I'm from the *Tarenton Lighter*. I'd like to get a picture of the six of you with your coach before the presentation."

"There'll be no pictures," Vanessa snapped. Mary Ellen had never seen her so upset. It did Mary Ellen's heart good.

"Get out of here!" Vanessa told him.

Al did not appreciate being ordered around. "What's your problem, girl?"

Vanessa stomped the floor and turned red. "I said, get out of here!"

Mary Ellen patted the fellow's arm. "I'll be there in a minute," she said sweetly.

The photographer pointed an angry finger at Vanessa. "*You* better look for another ride home." He stalked away.

"Where were we?" Mary Ellen said to Vanessa when they were alone again, as isolated as they could be in an auditorium crammed with two thousand people. "Oh, yes, I'm a liar. Does that mean you don't want me to come to any more of your parties?"

"I've a good mind to give that jerk your I.O.U. and let him take a picture of that!"

Mary Ellen casually reached inside her sweater pocket — she'd put it there for good luck — and pulled out a tightly folded list of Vanessa's hired help. A minute after Pres had taken possession of the list, she had lifted it from his pocket. She was going to have her revenge. "Give him a copy of this while you're at it," she said, handing her the creased photocopy. Vanessa stared at it in confusion.

"What is this!?" she demanded.

"Employees of Food for the Forgotten," Mary Ellen smiled. A long time from now, she knew, she would reflect back on this moment as one of the high points of her life.

"I don't know any of these people!"

"Didn't Cindy Dryer at Garrison Teen Agency mention that a teacher had called who wanted to send thank-you notes to your helpers?"

Light and darkness flashed simultaneously across Vanessa's face. She ripped the paper in half. "You have no proof now!" she shouted.

"I have twenty copies of that page you just

tore, each with the numbers of twenty people who will verify that they collected the money *you* took credit for collecting."

Vanessa's shoulders sagged, and her face lost its color. Mary Ellen would have felt pity for the girl if she hadn't been enjoying herself so much. Finally, Vanessa managed, "What do you want?"

Mary Ellen held up her hand and began to count off on her fingers. "First, I want the I.O.U. back."

"What else?"

"The money I already paid you."

"You *owe* me that!"

"I owe you nothing. I saw your expensive Swiss vase in J. C. Penney's. They couldn't give them away."

"What else?"

"A signed confession that you drugged me at the party."

"I can't give you that! I . . . I could go to jail!"

"I won't show it to anybody."

"How do I know you won't!?"

She mimicked Vanessa's line on the phone. "You'll have to trust me!" She added, "This is to keep you in line in the future. In exchange for all this, you get to remain the 'respected servant of the poor.' You have my word."

"I hate you, Mary Ellen. Is that all?"

"One other thing." She leaned over and whispered in Vanessa's ear. "Get out of here. You're spoiling my party."

The following Saturday night was clear and brisk. The runners gathered at the starting line at the far end of the stadium. Standing on the grass inside the track where the cross-country teams would soon pass, Olivia shivered from anxiety as well as the cold. Watching someone else compete was worse than competing yourself. Especially when that someone wasn't at full strength. Michael had said his foot was completely healed, but he couldn't hide the fact that he was still limping. She could see the coach positioning him next to David Clare, the Wickfield star. The stadium was filled to capacity and then some. If he lost tonight, few would know that it was his first loss in a long time.

On the drive home from Chetfield the week before, Michael had been his usual reserved self. Still unable to comprehend that they had won, she had been as talkative as a typical shock victim. Nevertheless, they had communicated — if not always with words — and by the time they had reached Tarenton, she had felt they were well on their way to becoming good friends. Whether they became more than that remained to be seen. For her part, she wanted *a lot* more. Michael was . . . he was Michael, a strong, silent mystery. She wondered what he wanted from her.

He hadn't taken her straight home. They had stopped in town at Kenny's Pizza where the other members of their squad were already eating. The celebration had been wild. When Olivia finally did get home, her mother had had the hardest time bawling her out while trying to congratulate her. It would be a long time before she forgot that Saturday.

The race began. Most of the audience stood as the brightly attired runners stampeded by. Olivia shouted Michael's name as loud as she could, but she doubted he heard with all the other cheering. As the runners completed the initial loop of the track and disappeared down the ramp, David Clare had gone to the front. Michael was lost somewhere in the pack. There was nothing she could do but wait.

Olivia turned away and walked toward the desks at the end of the finish line. She saw a truck towing the flowery homecoming queen presentation stand onto midfield. Unlike the usual halftimes, few in the crowd dashed off to the snack bar. Who would be chosen reigning queen for the next year was of great interest. Olivia wished she felt more excited about the event. She supposed the race was too distracting. Mary Ellen would almost certainly win the title — that is, if she and Angie could change into their gowns in time to make the ceremony. Mrs. Engborg had ordered that both of them were to remain in their uniforms and behave like cheerleaders, until the last second of the first half. At the moment, Mary Ellen and Angie were down in the girl's locker room trying to transform themselves from athletic young girls to sophisticated, elegant princesses. Olivia wouldn't have minded seeing that.

Pres looked down at the bouquet of roses in his hands, and glanced up at Patrick as both waited outside the girls' locker room for Mary Ellen to finish changing. Pres wondered if there wasn't room in his heart for "the other guy." He knew Mary Ellen was seeing Pat. And it hadn't mattered too much. Sure, Pres thought, she would look great on his arm and would enhance his image, but did he really care for her or was he simply looking to boost his own male ego? Her angel face made it hard to tell what she was really like. If he was honest with himself, he'd admit they didn't seem to have much in common.

Time will tell, he decided. There's no sense in worrying about it.

"Any sign of her coming out?" he called, taking the plunge and walking up to Patrick.

"I heard her fighting with Angie a minute ago," Patrick said. "Looks like the football team is going to have a long halftime."

They were so different. It wasn't only that Pres was rich and that Patrick drove a garbage truck. And it wasn't only that Pres was blond and smooth, and Patrick was dark and rugged. It was their attitudes and points of view toward life. Pres was uninterested in work and earning money, and Patrick was dedicated to it. Pres liked Mary Ellen because she looked good and made him look better. Patrick loved Mary Ellen because she was Mary Ellen.

They would have made miserable partners on a desert island. Five minutes went by and all they talked about was the game — Tarenton was losing, twenty-seven to ten — and the weather. Fortunately, Walt came by and proved an interesting distraction. He was with a short, cute Wickfield cheerleader. It was practically blasphemy, consorting with the enemy. In spite of himself, Pres was jealous. Walt's girl was a doll.

"Nicole, this is Pres," Walt said. "Pres's father owns half the city. And this gentleman is Patrick. His father keeps clean the half Pres's father doesn't own."

Nicole thought, along with Walt, that that was one of the finest jokes ever told. They were made for each other. When they were done laughing, Pres asked, "When and where did you two meet?"

"Last week at the finals," Walt said.

"*After* the finals," Nicole clarified. "I waited until he won before letting him see me."

That was good for another lengthy chuckle. If I went with Mary Ellen a year, Pres thought, I wouldn't be as close as these two are now. He watched with slight envy as the happy couple, arms interlocked, headed toward the shadows of the center of the school. About the time they disappeared, Nancy and Alex showed up.

"We just came from the hill behind the stands," Nancy said. "From there we could see the cross-country course as it runs by the lake. Michael's not doing so hot. He's back in fourth."

"I'm sorry to hear that," Pres said. "His foot must be too much of a handicap."

"I understand he has a strong finish," Alex added hopefully, his clothes more extravagant than usual: a blue top hat, a polka-dot shirt, black leather pants, and, of course, the earring. His band was the entertainment for the dance that was to be held in the gym immediately after the game. Mrs. Engborg had gotten his group the date.

Nancy nodded toward the locker room. "I don't suppose Mary Ellen and Angie have shown signs of appearing?"

Pres checked his watch. "Better tell them to hurry. Halftime is already half over."

Nancy released Alex's hand. "If I'm not out in five minutes," she said, "come to my rescue. Mary Ellen hates to be interrupted when she's putting on her makeup."

As Nancy walked into the locker room, she heard, "If you hadn't put on *my* dress in the first place," Mary Ellen scowled at Angie's reflection adjacent to hers in the mirror, "we wouldn't be as late as we are. How could you be so stupid?"

"But I still have on your dress," Angie said, applying her lip gloss. "We haven't lost a minute. Anyway, my dress is prettier than yours. I don't see what you're complaining about."

That was true. In fact, it was why she hadn't demanded that Angie get out of her gown. Of course, she wasn't going to admit that. "My mother made what you're wearing. She stayed up late every night this week to finish it. It has sentimental value. She'll be in the audience."

"They're both white and lacy. She'll never know the difference. I sure didn't." Angie reached for a candy bar in her purse. Mary Ellen stopped her.

"You are not going to eat chocolate in *my* dress!"

"But I'm hungry."

"Have a glass of water. There will be *no* stains on my dress."

"You're not queen yet. You can't order me around."

"If your humble maidservant may interrupt," Nancy said, coming through the open door, "your court is growing impatient."

"A minute," Mary Ellen said, wiping off most of the blush she had just applied. "Nancy, feed this animal that Snickers. It may touch her teeth and tongue — nothing else."

"Are you serious?" Nancy asked.

Opening her mouth wide, Angie nodded.

Five minutes later, when Mary Ellen got to the point where she felt she would need another hour to significantly improve her face, she pulled Angie away from her hand-fed candy. Since Nancy had come to hurry them up, Mary Ellen was surprised when she stopped them at the door.

"I wanted to wish you good luck," Nancy said.

"You can't wish us both good luck," Angie said. "We're competing against each other. Decide. Who are you going to root for — Mary Ellen or me?"

Shaking her head, Nancy said, "I don't care which of you gets it, as long as one of you beats Vanessa."

Mary Ellen realized it must have been difficult for Nancy to say that in light of her not having been elected to the court. She appreciated the support. A few weeks ago, when classes had just begun, the idea of being homecoming queen had been exciting, something that would add a special magic to the school year. Since then, it had become an obsession. She *had* to win. Battling with Vanessa had made the contest a life and death matter. If Vanessa won . . . best not to think about it.

"I don't care who beats her, either," Mary Ellen whispered (to no one) "as long as it's me."

The rise of the audience was like the crashing of a swift wave. One instant everyone was seated, and the next, thousands of spectators were on their feet screaming. Olivia turned toward the stadium entrance and gasped. David Clare had crested the ramp and was striding toward the track. Mentally, she began to count. Coach Riley had told her that Michael could make up ten seconds on the best runners in the state over the last quarter of a mile, he had such incredible natural speed. But she had passed eleven and was going on twelve when he bobbed out of the shadows. By then David was starting on the final loop of the track. As Michael charged onto the track, he was seventy yards behind the Wickfield star. In the blink of an eye, the gap shrunk to fifty yards.

"Go Michael!" Olivia screamed with thousands of others. The roar was deafening. Never had she heard such noise for a football game. Michael would have to revise his opinion of how boring these races were. "Go Michael!"

Going into the far bend, three quarters of the way home, David Clare glanced briefly over his shoulder. His shock upon seeing Michael closing was obvious. Now he knew it wasn't a sure thing, and the knowledge upset his rhythm. Michael, on the other hand, appeared to smooth out, shifting into his gazelle-like stretch. The gap closed to forty yards. They passed the halfway post and turned into the final curve . . . thirty yards between them.

"Faster!" Olivia screamed with half the city, the runners moving to the ribbon at the finish line. They had completed the final bend and were charging directly toward her. Michael would catch him, *if* he had the time.

"Michael!!!"

Eyes closed, Michael seemed to have slipped into another world. With fifty yards to go, he had still ten yards to make up. Somewhere he must have hoarded away the energy for a final burst. As David caught sight of the ribbon and began to lean toward it, Michael's feet literally flew off the ground. In three seconds, the space between them vanished, then reappeared, widening in reverse. Michael was in front! He was hitting the tape!

Olivia caught up with him at the end of the chute. He was bent over, his hands on his knees, fighting for air. Olivia stood over Michael with the number *1* stick in her hand. He appeared to recognize her feet and looked up, trying to smile.

"No sweat," he gasped.

"Can I get you anything?" she asked.

He nodded weakly, his head dropping back down.

"What?"

"Your arm," he whispered, trying to straighten. She gave him both arms and walked him out to the side of the track, where his sweats were draped over a hurdle. The crowd was still shouting his name. He was so drained, she had to help him get his sweatshirt over his head. She patted him on the back.

"You won." It meant more to her than her winning last Saturday.

He nodded, beginning to catch his breath. "Barely."

"You were great. You were fantastic!"

He squinted, surprised at her enthusiasm. "Yeah?"

Where her courage came from, she would never figure out. Stretching on her tiptoes, she kissed him firmly, saying, "You're the best."

For an instant he looked shocked, then he threw his head back and laughed like she never heard him laugh before. "Does this mean you'll go to the dance with me?"

"Do you like to dance?"

"No. But I like you."

"*Do you*?"

"Of course. That's why I went into the gym looking for you that morning. Didn't you know?"

Smiling, Olivia clasped his hands. "I wasn't sure." She forgot she had ever been ill, that she'd ever been lonely. Michael was making up for all those painful years.

CHAPTER

Vanessa was glad the race was over. Who cared who was the fastest runner? The football team certainly didn't. Only now as they returned to witness the announcement of the homecoming queen, the jersey-clad team formed to the left of the presentation stand. Vanessa saw Steve Dextrile wave, but did not wave back. He was no asset tonight, having led the football team through a miserable first half. She should probably dump him. All the assets in the world couldn't help her now; the votes were in and counted. Wishing she had x-ray vision, she stared at the vanilla envelope Principal Oetjen held in her hand. If her name wasn't typed on the little slip of paper inside that envelope, she was going to build a guillotine and introduce its blade to Al Scoly's neck. When she had called the *Tarenton Lighter* Wednesday morning, after opening the paper and not finding her smiling face in even the classified section, she had learned that the photographer had not delivered the roll of film with her UNICEF check presentation on it. Of course, he hadn't lost his snapshots of the cheerleading squad's "triumphant performance." All six of them had been on the front page, with Mary Ellen embracing the trophy like it belonged to her alone. It had been one rotten week, Vanessa thought.

Angie and Mary Ellen, carrying a dozen red roses each and wearing practically identical white gowns, finally showed up. Vanessa moved away, placing the other two girls — whatever their names were, she couldn't remember — between them. She had no intention of even looking at Mary Ellen, but Mrs. Oetjen gathered them in a half circle around the microphone and a certain amount of eye contact became unavoidable.

"Ladies and gentlemen!" Mrs. Oetjen's voice boomed through the stadium. "The moment you've all been waiting for! One of these five ladies is to be our new queen!" She introduced each of them — the two strangers were Sandra Quade and Terri Fisher — adding brief biographical highlights. There followed light applause while the principal fumbled for her glasses.

"This is the part I like," she smiled, playing with the envelope as if the rest of their lives didn't depend on what was inside it. She broke the seal and pulled out the folded yellow slip. She had trouble unfolding the piece of paper. Finally, however, she was able to read it. "Our new homecoming queen is. . . . !"

Mary Ellen closed her eyes and held her breath. A second that seemed an hour long crawled by. A hush settled over the stadium.

"ANGIE POLETTI!"

Angie's face broke into a huge grin.

Mrs. Oetjen extended a congratulatory hand toward Angie.

Sandra Quade and Terri Fisher both hugged Angie.

Last year's homecoming queen began to move forward, removing her crown and heading for Angie.

Like they had at the finish of the cross-country race, the crowd jumped to their feet, shouting "*Angie!*"

"No," Vanessa whispered. "No!"

"I can't believe it!" Angie shouted, laughing loudly.

While Angie stumbled through her acceptance speech, Mary Ellen, standing to the right, was silent and still as though in shock. She had wanted to be homecoming queen desperately. But she smiled faintly, cherishing one compensation — Vanessa Barlow had *lost.*

When Mrs. Oetjen had opened the envelope, Mary Ellen had braced herself for two possibilities: "Mary Ellen Kirkwood!" or "Vanessa Barlow!" When neither name was called, Mary Ellen found herself emotionally lost. Bitterness or jubilation would have been simple. But Angie was her teammate. Bitterness would have been inappropriate, and there was no sense pretending she felt jubilant. She tried to deny her wrenching disappointment.

I don't care, she thought. I don't care that much. I have my health, my family, my friends. I have everything, I've lost nothing.

All lies.

Mary Ellen closed her eyes and then looked at Angie. As soon as Angie was done with her speech, she would have to tell her how happy she was for her. It would hurt and would be a lie but it would *have* to be done.

When Mrs. Oetjen had called her name Angie had thought for an instant that it was like the Miss America contest, where the runner-ups were announced first. Then, when the truth had finally sunk in, she had been more than pleased and more than a little surprised.

Only one regret blemished her crowning— Mary Ellen had lost. Mary Ellen had really deserved to win. She had class, beauty, and many other "royal" qualities.

Patrick, watching Angie and Mary Ellen, almost cried for Mary Ellen. He knew why Angie had won. Why her dazzling smile and natural friendliness had won the hearts and minds of the student body. But what was Mary Ellen feeling?

Nancy held her breath when the announcement of the homecoming queen was made. She was surprised, without a doubt. She looked over at Mary Ellen and saw the disappointment and jealousy on her face. Then she looked at Vanessa and saw the rage and fury. Now what? Nancy thought. How will Mary Ellen work with Angie for the rest of the year? And what will Vanessa do next to hurt us . . . to try and tear us apart?

Nancy heard Angie say into the microphone,

"Please, I want my squad up here with me . . . all of them."

Mrs. Oetjen signaled for the five cheerleaders to join Angie at the mike. Awkwardly, they formed a semi-circle around Angie. Angie tried to hug them all at once, and suddenly the atmosphere changed and they *were* hugging and kissing each other. Mary Ellen kissed Angie's cheek and whispered, "We beat Vanessa. That's what counts." And she meant it . . . at least for the moment.

The crowd roared its approval as the squad waved and blew kisses. Then the six of them formed the letter T, Angie and Mary Ellen's white dresses blowing in the night wind. Patrick and Alex raced out on the field, carrying red pompons that the squad took and raised high in their hands.

Let this last, Nancy thought. Let us stay like this forever. She knew it wasn't possible, but for now tomorrow didn't matter.

Will Patrick force Mary Ellen to choose between him and Pres? Read Cheerleaders #3, RUMORS.

Feuding
by Lisa Norby
(*April*)

Tensions are high among the squad members when Nancy and Olivia fall for the same boy ... and Vanessa supplies the spark that sets the fireworks in action!

All the Way
by Caroline B. Cooney
(*May*)

Nancy finds new love with the captain of the basketball team... Tarenton's arch rival, that is! As the race between the two schools comes down to the wire, Nancy finds herself torn. Can she remain loyal to Tarenton High?

Splitting
by Jennifer Sarasin
(*June*)

Pres has had it! He wants out of his parents' home–even if it means getting kicked off the squad. Thanks to Vanessa, he just might be...

Everything you've always wanted...and more!

from Scholastic Inc. $2.25 each